What Pearl Harbor Wrought

Photo of Heart Mountain Internment Camp by Yoshio Okumoto from the collection of Bacon Sakatani.

Akio Konoshima

D1475177

Plain View Press
P.O. 42255
Austin, TX 78704

plainviewpress.net
pk@plainviewpress.net
512-441-2452

ISBN: 978-1-935514-68-8
Library of Congress Number: 2010932906

Cover art: *Lonely Camp* by Chizuko Judy Sugita de Quieroz from her book *Camp Days: 1942-1945* available at: www.artbychiz.com/campdays_book.html.

Cover design by Susan Bright.

This episodic novel is dedicated to the Issei. They were denied the equality promised by the U.S. Constitution, denied naturalization rights, suffered the loss of sons and daughters and homes, farms. businesses, during WWII, even their freedom. Yet, their faith in America endured, and those fortunate to live that long, saw their off-springs succeed in all aspects of American life — as members of Congress, cabinet secretaries, army generals, state governors, business leaders, college presidents, various professions and as just good citizens. God Bless Their Souls.

Contents

The author accepting the award as a finalist in the short story contest at the National Press Club in Washington, D.C., October 19, 1993, for his entry "Sister."

Introduction

The title of this episodic novel, *What Pearl Harbor Wrought*, comes from the fact that it was the trauma of the Japanese attack on December 7, 1941, that shaped the lives of the author and so many others of the World War II generation – those of Japanese Americans – in its own unique way.

Other minorities also faced questions on their rights and identity as Americans. For the *Nikkei*, however, the questions became particularly poignant during World War II when all persons with Japanese blood, be they citizens or not, were removed from their homes on the U.S. West Coast and detained in barbed-wired "relocation centers" in desolate parts of America. Dreams were shattered, homes were lost, livelihoods taken away.

This episodic novel is based on the author's observations while growing up in California, experiencing the trauma of Pearl Harbor and the internment, and then serving in the U.S. Army in occupied Japan and in the Korean conflict. This was followed by a return to Tokyo as a civilian to try to be but realizing that he could not be "just another Japanese," then life in London, where again he experienced the uniqueness of being – in the eyes of others – neither fully "American" nor fully "Japanese."

The author hopes his efforts will give his children and grandchildren a sense of their heritage.

Acknowledgments

Credit for completion of this work should go to the Writer's Center in Bethesda, Maryland, whose workshops I have been attending for more years than I'd like to mention.

My special thanks go to the Center's founders and instructors Al Lefcowitz and Tom Allen; plus instructors Sid Silkin, Joyce Kornblatt and others as well as the participants of the workshops whose names I have forgotten but whose constructive criticism was very much appreciated.

Earlier inspiration which took decades for fruition came in the late 1930's and early1940's from my high school English IV teachers, a Ms. Read and a Mr. Hazeltine; English composition professor Dr. Josephine Chandler at what was then San Jose State College, and short story classes with the late Helen C. White at the University of Wisconsin in Madison.

I give a great deal of credit too, to the writers of Japanese American history whose works have been especially helpful for recalling and putting into perspective the events which shaped our lives. They include Michi Weglyn, author of *Years of Infamy*; Brian Niiya, editor of *Japanese American History*; Jean Wakatsuki and James D. Houston, co-authors of *Farewell to Manzanar*, the late journalist Bill Hosokawa, and other Asian American writers such as Amy Tan, Gus Lee, David Mura, and Wakako Yamaguchi, whose works made me want to tell some of my own stories.

Special thanks go to Justin Shen and his most patient and gracious wife, Lily Yue, whose expertise with the computer hand-walked the author through the many intricacies of the computer which many of the author's generation find almost impossible to figure out.

This novel was inspired by the author's parents, both now long dead. Special thanks go to my wife Lida Ling Allen, whose love and support has made this book possible.

Glossary

Editor's note: Japanese words were used throughout this collection to try to maintain the bilingual atmosphere that prevailed in most of the situations. When read in context the meanings of these words should be clear. However, listed below are some of the words more commonly used:

Nikkei: Japanese-American or Japanese American since the term can be used either as a noun or an adjective, and can be either singular or plural.

Issei: The first generation designating people born in Japan who immigrated to America and were barred from naturalization by law until 1953.

Nisei: The second generation, children of the *issei* who were born in America and thus, U.S. citizens.

Kibei: Nisei who were sent to Japan for a substantial part of their early education and then returned to America.

Shinpai: Worry. The suffix *"-nai"* makes the word negative, thus *shinpai-nai* means not to worry.

Tanka: A Japanese verse form of 31 syllables as opposed to the more familiar *haiku* which is composed of 17 syllables.

Sho-ga-nai: It can't be helped.

Nappa: sometimes translated "greens" or "Chinese cabbage," *Take-no-ko:* bamboo shoots, *konnyaku:* a paste made from a tuberous root, are Japanese foodstuff, and are left untranslated though they may never become as familiar to the American reader as "tofu."

Chapter One
Our Farm
(Part I)

Dec. 7, 1941: Local authorities and the FBI begin to round up the Issei leadership of the Japanese American communities in Hawaii and on the mainland. Within 48 hours 1,291 Issei are in custody, held under no formal charges and contact with their families forbidden. (Brian Niiya, Editor, Japanese American History, the Japanese American National Museum, page 53)

Feb. 19, 1942: President Roosevelt signs Executive Order 9066, which allows military authorities to exclude anyone from anywhere without trial or hearings. (ibid, page 55)

O

It was late December, 1934. But for Jo, 10-years-old going on to 11, the approaching Christmas was overshadowed by a far more momentous event. The family — his mother and father, an older sister, two older brothers, and two younger sisters — was moving from rented acreage to a farm that was to be their own.

On the day of the move (some of the household goods and farming equipment had already been hauled ahead), Jo and his brother, Tak, rode on the back of the old Ford Model A pickup, driven by his father. The mother sat up front with the father. The other children were driving in the family's black, cloth-covered Ford Model T.

Jo's excitement bubbled over while they were still on the Bayshore Highway, two or so miles from the farm.

"That's it. That's our place," Tak said, grabbing the backboard and standing up as he pointed to a cluster of trees and buildings just beyond a grove of eucalyptus trees.

Jo stood and saw a barn with weathered gray sides and a sagging shingled roof, two tall pine trees, and then a house, windmill, and several expansive oaks above the low outline of orchards in the background. Though the winter air was cold, the cluster of buildings and the trees seemed warm; the vigorous twirling of the metal blades of the windmill added to the welcome.

His brother had been to the farm earlier when furniture and equipment were moved and though he repeated for about the tenth time his list of what was on the farm, Jo still listened in awe. The farm had fruit trees of all types — peach, cherry, plum, apricot, pear, fig, even loquat and tiny lemon and orange trees — in addition to almonds and walnuts; big oaks for climbing; bee hives by the barn; and rabbits, squirrels, pheasants, doves, owls, even a sea hawk which flew in from the Bay; and a deep irrigation well surrounded by grape vines.

As the winter wind cut across their faces, Jo's imagination raced ahead to when the fruits would be ripe: summer and he would be up the fig tree, feeling the brush of fuzzy leaves against his arms, seeing the milky sap ooze from the stems of plump, dark fruit as they were picked; tasting their fresh sweetness.

"Gee," Jo kept saying, "gee."

The truck turned off of the highway onto a two-lane paved road; then after several minutes, onto a long dirt road leading into the farm. On one side grayish-barked walnut trees and purple-hued prune trees stood in alternate rows, dew dripping from their branches onto Indian grass covering the orchard floor. On the other side, a dozen or so cows in an open corral gave off steam from their warm, moist bodies as they calmly chewed cud and watched.

The two jumped off of the pickup even before it came to a full stop. Jo ran, looking up at the two pine trees which stood by the side of the barn — one so old it had dark green needles only in tufts at its very top; the other with branches heavy with shaggy needles almost touching the ground. Above the gray, weather-worn side of the barn itself, mud swallows' nests pushed against each other under the eaves.

In the barn the two clambered over old straw bales to the south loft; then down through a trap door to six or seven stalls. Dry leather blinders and light harness still hung from wooden pegs. The feed troughs contained scattered left-over barley and worn salt blocks. Cobwebs seemed to cover everything, and the cobwebs themselves were so covered with dust even the spiders did not seem to live there anymore. But in his mind, Jo pictured trim, prancing carriage and riding horses with glistening hides which once must have lived there.

"Oi. *Shigoto* — there's work to be done," their father called. Though his father's voice was gruff, coming out of the barn Jo caught the glimpse of a smile as his father turned toward his mother, who, in her home-made, unbleached denim work pants and cotton bonnet, was clearing weeds along the path to the house.

Jo and Tak carried cartons of clothes, bedding, and pots and pans from the pickup into the house, and shovels, hoes, pruning saws and black rubber irrigation boots to a nearby shed. A garage, he could hear his father saying to his mother, could be set up under the nearby valley oaks. Dahlias, she replied, could be planted in the sunny side of the garden. Flowering cherry trees would do well in front of the house; the prune trees nearby could be grafted with other fruit; an old oak stump on the north side of the house could be the centerpiece for a rock garden. They talked as excited as he.

Jo and his brother had no time to return to the barn that day. It didn't matter, they could continue their exploration the next day, or the day after that, or whenever they wanted — the farm was theirs.

From that first day, work never ceased. The prune trees were cut down because the price of prunes was too low to harvest; the wood stored under the oak trees for later use to heat the outdoor Japanese-style bath. The Scarinos, Swiss-Italians neighbors who had a Caterpillar, were hired to pull up the stumps, then plow and disc the cleared areas. In the spring a patch of pole peas was the first crop harvested. Several acres of raspberries and loganberries were planted.

As time allowed, Jo and his brothers swept the south loft of the barn clean, then set up horizontal bars and a swing underneath the rafters. They found an owls' nest in the north loft. Though they could never creep up softly enough to see the birds actually sitting there, on moonlit nights Jo often caught glimpses of the owls as they zig-zagged silently in the air in search of prey on the darkened ground or heard the owls' high-pitched screech.

Trees were planted around the house and the prune trees grafted; the rock garden was started; dahlias and roses were the first flowers planted on the sunny side of the house. Later, a petrified log was added as the rock garden's centerpiece. Jo's father spotted the log, covered with seaweed and barnacles, among slippery rocks at the seashore near Pescadero on an abalone hunt during an extra low tide. Must have been in a prehistoric forest fire, his father said. Charcoal from its bark had crystallized, forming a crust which some day might have become black diamonds. The log made the garden a whole as the garden made the house their home.

A Saturday night. It rained all day and was still drizzling at supper time. Inside the house was warm. Nakano-san had come over. He and Jo's father sat at the edge of the kerosene stove, moved from its wall position closer to the kitchen table, so that the two men could pick, Japanese-style, from the simmering *sukiyaki*. The meat included beef exchanged for a crate of celery with a Chinese butcher in San Jose, and a pheasant, shot a few days earlier in the raspberry patch. The *napa, negi,* bell peppers and other vegetables came either from his mother's garden or from the field. The smell and steam of food cooking in the soy sauce filled the room.

The children sat at the table; their mother at the stove, adding meat and vegetables to the frying pan as needed, filling the plates, and being hostess to the father and his guest. Both had red faces from beer and *sake*. His father had even coaxed his mother into having a few sips of the *sake*. They laughed and talked.

Jo was intent on eating. He had heard the stories his parents told numerous times before — about the original plans for coming to America representing a paper-pulp trading company; the 1923 Tokyo earthquake which destroyed the company's stocks; the decision to emigrate anyway and chance it on their own. They talked about Bacon Island in the delta area of California where the family first settled: his father about the fishing and hunting there; his mother about the terror the river had for her after Jo's near drowning.

The farm they were now on was being bought on a ten-year mortgage, Jo knew. His family farmed 16 acres; their neighbors, the Kiyono's, the other 24. Jo had always assumed that the portion they farmed was theirs, once the mortgage was paid off. This gave him comfort; no one was their landlord or boss.

Jo was about to refill his rice bowl, when he heard his father mention the mortgage payment. He'd go to the bank Monday to get the money for the Kiyonos' eldest son, Kenji, Jo's father said.

"Does Kenji take the money to the finance company for us?" Jo, a bit puzzled, asked his brother Tak.

"No," Tak said. "We pay Kenji. Kenji pays the mortgage company."

"I don't understand," Jo said.

"Dummy," Tak said. "The farm can't be under our name."

"Why?"

"We aren't citizens. You can't be. I can't be. Orientals can't become U.S. citizens unless they're born here. U.S. law says so. California law says you can't own land in the state unless you're a U.S. citizen."

"Oh?"

"Uh huh. That's why it's under Kenji's name, but it's the same as being ours. We're paying the mortgage and taxes and things like that. We can't own it legally, that's all."

"Ours but not ours?" Jo asked.

"Something like that," Tak said, then shrugged.

"But it has to be ours, only ours," Jo protested. "Suppose...," but he knew then that what he thought was theirs, really was not. Scrambling on top of the bales of hay in the barn, climbing the oaks, watching the honey bees go in and out of their hives, inspecting the fruit trees — somehow things would not be as much fun any more.

○

"Whoa," Kisa shouted as he restrained the horse so he could unhook the plow. They had just finished plowing the raspberry patch. The horse wanted to get back to the barn for its hay and the warmth of the stable. It was sunny, but cold. Frost still showed on the shaded areas of the ground, but it was not deep enough to prevent working the soil. In the afternoon, they could weed areas around the berry bushes.

The animal is like a petulant child, Kisa mused as the horse kept pulling on the reins. Kisa had to walk on his heels to slow the pace on their way back to the barn.

Coming to America had been a gamble. Committing themselves to a farm they could not legally own was an additional gamble.

But at least after six years — four years still remained on the mortgage — the farm now clearly reflected the family's efforts and wishes. As he followed the path through the walnut orchard toward the barn, he could spot which trees he had grown from seed (black walnuts later grafted with English walnuts) to replace the older trees of the original orchard. Through proper pruning and irrigating, he had made the orchard productive again. Beyond the barn, bamboo now screened off the bathhouse and the outhouse. Nearby, the bare branches of the Shanghai peaches and Manchurian apricots he had grafted onto the trunks of prune trees reached skyward.

For all practical purposes, the farm was theirs even though, at times, Kisa had to wonder if they would be able to pay their share of the mortgage. He worried, for example, when string beans sold for a cent and a half a pound, or lettuce at 50 cents a crate. Such prices were too low to even meet the cost of trucking the produce to the San Francisco wholesale market. But with the war in Europe the depression soon had to be over.

Their agreement with the Kiyono family was a matter of trust between two Japanese families. Only the lines on the plat marking the areas each family would farm was put on paper. The two families shared a common well and pump to irrigate the fields, the barn to house their two horses and store the hay, and the windmill which drew drinking water for the two households from a second well. Otherwise they operated independently.

Kisa planned to eventually to put their share of the farm under the name of one of his two U.S.-born daughters. Until then he would have to live with what he had.

As he walked, Kisa thought back to when he was a university student in Kyoto and the inspiration he got when first studying the U.S. constitution. His first impression was tarnished a short time later when Japanese children were barred from San Francisco's public schools, but he still believed in what he thought could be ideal. He rationalized, blamed that action on the city's school board, not the country as a whole.

Even with the blatant racial inequities he found once he arrived in America, he still felt fortunate he had left Japan when he did.

In Japan he taught at an emigrants' school. His courses covered the basic economics, customs and various farming methods in Latin America that prepared the would-be emigrants for the countries they were destined for. He had worked his way through both senior high school and college. For years he got up a 4:30 a.m. each day to deliver milk and often was too tired to even stay awake in class. At times he was envious, at other times contemptuous, of fellow students, usually from well-off families, who seemed to spend more time playing than studying while he had to struggle to make ends meet. He identified himself with the working poor, made friends with like-minded students, some of whom were considered radical leftists in the Japan of that time. His political outlook did not change when he became a teacher and even led to his being interrogated by the Japanese military police — the *Kempei Tai* — for equating Japanese incursions on the China mainland with European colonialism. With the military gaining more and more control in Japan after he had left, he had been warned by friends in Tokyo that he faced arrest if he did return to Japan.

Thinking of the military, Kisa wondered what moves they had planned next. U.S.-Japanese relations already seemed at a breaking point.

A quick look at the sun told him it was almost noon. After watering and feeding the horse, he hurriedly walked to the house, entering through the front door into the parlor where the radio was, to catch the 12 o'clock newscast. Normally, he would wash up at the outdoor faucet at the back of the house. The talks between Kurusu, Japan's special envoy, and Japanese ambassador Nomura on one side, with U.S. officials were scheduled for the morning in Washington, D.C. and would already have taken place.

Kisa listened impatiently as the newscast was interrupted by static and messages to and from the control tower at nearby Moffet Field and training flights overhead. During one of these radio interruptions, Kisa heard the news: "Attack...Pearl Harbor...Japanese planes..."

Kisa listened, stunned. The newscast reported that a special session of Congress was to be convened the next day to declare a state of war, but did not give further details of the attack.

As he steadied himself, Kisa moved toward the kitchen, where his wife, Yoshi, was washing vegetables in the sink. She turned as she sensed his presence.

"*Nanka* — something wrong?" Yoshi asked.

"*Uh-senso* ... A war...," he started to say, unable to hide his anxiety.

"*Ara* ...," she replied, then, not turning back to the sink, just looked, searching his face.

A matter of seconds, but in those moments Kisa's emotions welled. She stood there, her hair tied in a bun behind her head, her brown eyes still searching, faint lines showing on her sun-tanned face. He also saw her faded blue cotton blouse, the corduroy work pants, heavy socks, the canvas rubber-soled shoes — life had not been easy.

He and she rarely showed their emotions, even when they were alone. "*Otona no yo ni* — act as an adult," she would tease if he showed too much affection.

But now his immediate instinct was to seek as well as give solace. Their world was about to collapse. He moved close to her, ignored her wet hands as he circled her with his arms, and held her tight, saying nothing. He could smell her hair, also the green onions in the sink.

Yoshi broke their silence. "*Ma shikari shinai to* — remain steadfast; we'll have to," she said, turning back to the sink as Kisa returned to the radio.

Kisa was still in a swirl of emotions when he heard his two younger sons coming in from the field. They already had heard the news from a neighbor, and soon joined him at the radio.

In spite of the run-ins Kisa had had with the *Kempei-Tai*, something he never mentioned to his sons, he had often talked to them about being

Japanese and what he thought ought to be Japan's place in the world. Japan was, he'd note, the first non-white nation to win a war against a European power, the first to thwart attempts of colonialism on its own shores, and above all, the nation destined to "free Asia for Asians."

Now, though, as they stood huddled around the radio, Kisa did not know what to say to his sons. Japan had attacked America. Wet-eyed, he remained silent.

His sons noticed, avoided eye contact.

The next day, Kisa drove to the Japanese language school in Mountain View, an unofficial community center, to learn more of what was happening to those of the local Japanese community. The radio newscasts said a string of arrests of leaders of the Japanese communities had taken place within hours of the news about Pearl Harbor.

Kisa was anxious to talk to Mr. Morita, the teacher at the Japanese language school, who knew of most of the Japanese families within the surrounding area. But when Kisa got to the school he learned that not only Morita-san, but Mr. Takeda, head of the local Japanese Association; Reverend Tsuda, the minister at the Buddhist church, and the directors of the local *kendo* (Japanese fencing) and *judo* clubs had already been arrested.

Kisa saw Mrs. Morita just briefly. She said two men in plain clothes had come shortly afternoon, identified themselves as with the FBI, then took her husband away, allowing him to take only some clothing and a toilet kit.

"They wouldn't say when or how I could contact him; wouldn't even tell me where they were taking him," she said, finally showing a trace of tears. "I'm worried. I know he's worried. What are they going to do to us? Our children? Ichiro, our oldest, is only eight years old; the other two still babies."

"They should let you know something soon," Kisa said to try to calm her fears, though he had no way of knowing any more than she did.

Reverend Osano, the minister who served the three Japanese Methodist churches in San Jose, Mountain View and Palo Alto, also was at the school but just shrugged when asked about the arrests. "They still might pick me up. Maybe being a Christian helps. Who knows?" was all he could say.

Kisa left the language school mulling over what he had heard as he drove home to beat the dusk to dawn curfew imposed for all Japanese. He learned nothing new officially on what he and the other Japanese should or should not do. But he was disturbed.

He was told that Kato-san, a gardener Kisa had worked with in Los Altos who was a highly devoted Christian, took rat poison because he felt all was lost. Fortunately, the man did not die though he remained hospitalized. There were whispers that Suzuki, a farmer with eleven children, had castrated himself because of his depression and possibly a guilt feeling for having had so many children.

Kisa shook his head as he thought of his two friends. He could understand their feeling of despair. Still, their suffering could have been avoided. Surely someone could have or should have talked to them out of such drastic action.

Kisa was not an official or leader of any of the community groups nor was he doing any formal teaching as he had when they first came to America. He remained on edge, however, He was among the few adults of the community with a college degree; many people knew he had been a school teacher in Japan.

He could not hide his nervousness from the children. Less than a week later, his son Jo sat listening to the radio newscast — Japanese submarines were reported lurking offshore near San Francisco Bay. Kisa had gone outside to check to make sure that no light was leaking out through the shaded windows. He had just returned to the parlor to catch the news himself, when the son lifted the corner of a shade to peek out to see if the blackout was as full as the radio reported. The catch on the shade then suddenly let go and the entire shade, its roller spring still new, twirled up with a snap, leaving the window bare. In horror, Kisa rushed to the window, pushing Jo aside, and pulled the shade down again. Even as he moved, Kisa realized that his son already was starting to rise to do the same.

Kisa was about to scold, but stopped. It was a simple accident. But what if someone had seen it, accuse them of sending out some sort signal. Kisa knew, on second thought, that his reaction when the shade snapped up was ridiculous.

Kisa's instinct told him that if the FBI or the sheriff's office came, they would not worry about evidence if they had decided to take him away. He was determined, though, to get rid of anything that might be an excuse for arresting him.

Kisa had no expensive camera nor a short-wave radio which, along with guns or weapons of any sort, were declared contraband for any Japanese and were supposed to be turned in at the sheriff's office. Kisa had a 12-gauge shotgun and two 22-caliber rifles, however. He kept the shotgun, a late model which could hold five shells, polished and well-oiled. It was a toy with which he had spent many early morning hours stalking pheasants or rabbits while inspecting the fields. He felt too attached to it to simply turn it in or even to sell; finally decided just to give the shotgun and the two rifles to his Swiss-Italian neighbor, who often was a fishing and hunting companion.

In the back of the bedroom closet, Yoshi had a steamer trunk full of old clothes, papers, their passports, photos, and other family memorabilia. While the children were at school (he didn't want them to see what he was going to do), he and Yoshi carried the trunk to a fire he had lit in the make-shift barbecue pit (basically some bricks set around a hole in the ground) in the back of the house.

Nostalgia mixed with regret as Yoshi lifted each item from the trunk, passed it to Kisa to decide if it should be thrown onto flames. Two school uniforms, one light gray for summer and the other black for winter, might be mistaken as something military, Kisa thought, and so threw them on the fire. As they smoldered, then burst into flames, he recalled the long chats they had while she would be sewing on a button or mending a tear.

An old class picture, taken while Kisa was at Seijo Senior High School in Tokyo was still in its cardboard frame. Many of the teachers, reserved officers of the Imperial Japanese Army, were in uniform. Though the school prepared students for the Imperial Military Academy, Kisa was enrolled there simply because the school was the best among those which accepted his application. He never had any intention of joining the military. The picture might give the opposite impression.

As he watched the picture burn, out of the corner of his eyes Kisa saw Yoshi's hands pause as she picked up a certificate of some sort. The paper was brown with age, but its gold seal still shiny. As she noticed him look, she handed it over to him quickly, as if it were something it hurt to hold.

The script on the certificate, with Yoshi's name carefully brushed in, still was legible though faded, and simply read, "First Prize. National Calligraphy Competition," then gave the date, the 36th Year of Meiji (1904). The competition was held annually in each school throughout the Japanese national public school system. Yoshi had won it in her grade school in Honjo. Kisa knew that she prized the certificate.

Would the FBI take it for something else? Should it be burned? Kisa was not sure.

Before he could make up his mind, however, Yoshi grabbed it from his hands and threw it on the fire herself.

"*Sonna mono* — that sort of thing, who needs it," she said.

Though it happened only in a matter of seconds, when Yoshi picked up the certificate to hand to Kisa, time for Yoshi suddenly stood still. As the musty smell of burning paper mixed with the sharp odor of the burning cotton, Yoshi could clearly recall the late spring day when she was awarded the certificate.

She was sitting with the other girls in her class at the final school assembly for the semester. The boys sat on the other side of the aisle. Yoshi was relaxed since all of the final examinations were over. Though the grades still had not be given out, she was confident she had not done badly. Entries to the Emperor's calligraphy contest had been submitted long ago, and she had forgotten about it; the idea of winning never even having crossed her mind.

When her name was announced, she was stunned. She just sat, embarrassed, as all the eyes in the assembly hall suddenly turned towards her. She sat until told by the kindly principal that she should join him on the stage to receive the prize. She remembered keeping her eyes down as she walked over the unpainted wooden floor of the hall, noticing the grain of each pine board, its surface worn down over the years by the tread of students' feet; and hearing the whispers of the other students, some apparently as surprised as she was, some just envious. On the stage she was too excited to remember all the details, only that she was further embarrassed as the principal read notes on what the prize meant.

But as she stood on the stage, a change took place in her own mind. She was 12 years old then, in the seventh grade. One more year of elementary school and she would have completed the eight years of compulsory education then required of all children in Japan. Normally, in Japan of that period, her formal schooling would have been over the following year. At times she had had vague thoughts of continuing her education. But until then, such thoughts were only daydreams. Private girls schools, even for secondary education, were meant only for the elite and certainly too expensive for her family.

However, she remembered thinking — she had not expected to win the Emperor's award, yet she had, the sole winner in the entire school. Why not seriously try for further schooling regardless of the odds? At that moment, what had been a daydream became a goal.

Later, she did a lot of searching in the school and town libraries and elsewhere, but could find nothing suitable. About the same time, her parents, though vague about the details, were hinting that discussions with possible in-laws-to-be already had taken place.

She had almost given up her quest for further schooling, when she learned about a Workers' School in Tokyo where girls could work while enrolled to pay for their education. Though it took a year, her application was accepted. But for the Worker's School, she may have never left Honjo, her home town, nor ever met Kisa; probably would never...

She watched the fire engulf the certificate; the paper curl, then turned from brown to black; then as the flames consumed it, fall away as ashes. Before the gold seal — the last part of the certificate to burn — disappeared, she quickly reached into the trunk for the next item. They had no time to be sentimental.

Yoshi next picked up an inch-thick manuscript with a purple cloth cover, bound with a white silk cord. Seeing it, Kisa smiled to himself. He had rewritten the report several times, trying to leaven its statistics with personal accounts of the people he had interviewed. The study surveyed conditions that prevailed for Japanese communities in the Philippines, Southeast Asia, the Indian subcontinent, South Africa, and then the various countries of Latin America and looked into the possibilities for further emigration. He did the study for the old *Shokumin Gakko* (Emigrants' School) at *Ike-no-ue*, then a suburb of Greater Tokyo, where he had taught, but the Japanese Education Ministry printed it as well. The inside cover page had the official ministry seal and at the bottom Kisa's name and *hanko* — personal seal.

The report was more than just numbers, types of work being done, relative incomes, schools and other details he had sought; it was also like a diary. He was tempted to thumb through the report, refresh his memory, but instead threw it into the fire.

The report was 20 or so years old, far out of date. But what if the FBI or the sheriff's office found it and gave it to the press. Kisa could almost see the headlines it might make: "Local Jap Farmer Arrested, Official Study of Potential Fifth Column Resources Discovered During House Search." It seemed ridiculous, but Kisa knew it was all too possible.

The fire shot up as it was fed the pages. For Kisa, the flames, in miniature, were like those of the fires that swept Tokyo following the great earthquake of 1923. The quake and the flames then had changed the whole course of his and his family's lives. The war was bringing about even bigger change.

On Dec. 7, 1941, Jo was just one month shy of being 18 years old. At that age, he was fascinated as he followed the major events and the people involved in a changing world. Munich, then the war in Europe; the Marco Polo Bridge incident and the Japanese invasion of China; the sinking by the Japanese of the U.S.S. Panay; the Japanese move into Indo-China with the fall of France; America's economic embargo on trade with Japan; Hitler, Mussolini, Chamberlain, Churchill, Konoye, Tojo — Jo's pulse would quicken as he read the news.

Reading the news, however, was like reading history. These were events which seemed remote and not directly influencing his life.

Jo and his next oldest brother, Tak, learned of Pearl Harbor from the neighbor's younger son, Harry, as they were coming in from the field for lunch.

"Hey," Harry shouted across the yard, "We're at war. They've bombed Pearl Harbor."

"Who?"

"The Japanese."

It was the way the words were said; the look on Harry's face; the look on his brother's. No one had to say any more. Their looks indicated the same question: what's going to happen to us now? They knew, Jo knew, the news was no longer just about things remote.

On the Monday following the attack on Pearl Harbor, Jo took the train into San Jose to attend his classes at the state college there. He tried to act as if it were any normal Monday. On the train, Jo and the conductor who often was on the early morning run, exchanged their usual "good mornings." The other passengers seemed no different than usual. At school, though, the whole campus was bustling. Everyone, of course, was talking about the war — the National Guard units being called up, who among the students and teachers were in the reserves, where to go to volunteer, rumors about the damage the Japanese attack did to the U.S. Pacific Fleet.

Jo did not join any of these conversations. Often as he approached, voices were lowered and looks avoided. Ordinarily, at noon he would join a group of about a half dozen others from the same engineering physics class on a bench to eat lunch. That Monday and for the rest of the week, Jo ate his lunch alone, standing on an outdoor corridor overlooking the quadrangle to the main building on the college campus.

He was angered and embarrassed by Pearl Harbor. President Roosevelt's declaration of "The Day of Infamy" re-echoed in Jo's mind as the news media fanned the flames of anti-Japanese venom. Jo, though, would not join the chorus. Some of the Nisei he knew spoke of the "Goddamn Japs," voiced hatred in much stronger terms. He wondered, though, if they weren't protesting too loudly to show how "American" they were; maybe trying too hard to be non-Japanese in the eyes of people who could not see them as anything else but Japanese. Were the *Nisei* supposed to hate their mothers and fathers? Were they supposed to hate themselves? Jo even heard one Nisei student ask other Nisei, "Don't we know any *Issei* who's a spy so we can turn him in?" — like sacrificing one of their own to feed the frenzy.

Jo was shy and unobtrusive, said little even when with a Nisei group. Now, he didn't know how or with whom to share any thoughts about the war.

Near the end of the first week, Jo, still alone, was again eating his lunch on the outdoor corridor overlooking the quadrangle, when he felt a hand on his shoulders and a voice say, "Hey. Keep your chin up. Maybe it's not that bad."

Jo turned to see Dr. Meyer, his calculus professor. The man — slim, always neatly dressed in pin-striped blue suit, wearing rimless glasses — gave Jo a smile and went on his way. Jo realized then that standing there alone, he, Jo, must have presented quite a desolate figure.

The man's hand on Jo's shoulders woke Jo up. Whatever was going to happen, would happen, but in the meantime he would try again to concentrate on his studies.

Though President Roosevelt issued his executive order in February, it was May before the official notice of the evacuation was tacked up on the utility pole above the family's silver-colored mailbox. Jo didn't even bother to read it. The radio and newspapers already had reported the news, some playing the news up as a big triumph; for who or for what, Jo wondered.

During the wait for the official notification, Jo's oldest sister, Miyo, had gotten married and, to escape incarceration, had moved to St. Louis, where her husband was to finish dental school. None of the family could attend the wedding. The older brother returned from Berkeley to be with the family.

Over those weeks, the family prepared the fields for spring planning then dug new irrigation ditches as the dry season approached so that Frank Belli, a truck driver and long-time friend of the Kiyonos, could move in to run the farm until the families could return.

The day the family left the farm was warm and sunny, an extra bright spring day. All nature gave promise of the summer to come. The sky was clear blue; blackbirds and robins tilted their heads as they listened in their hunt for worms in the moist ground; the gnarled branches of the oak trees around the yard swayed in a gentle breeze. In the garden, early blooming Japanese morning glories spread their purple flowers wide into the sun; the green grass smelled fresh. A yellow-winged flicker, whose wing beats came in short bursts, rose and fell as it flew by.

Jo watched his mother's face as she stood beside the pickup giving the home a last look before getting on. New owners would take over the truck at the train station in Mountain View where the evacuees in the area were to assemble. His mother wore her Sunday dress, of loose-fitting dark non-lustrous silk, and a matching hat. She wore no makeup, but her face stood out — flat nose, tanned high cheeks, thinning eyebrows with a bit of gray, dark eyes. He looked at the face, wondered. Did she feel loss? Sorrow? Bitterness? Anger? Jo could not tell. The face remained calm.

As the pickup bumped along the dirt driveway, the house, the garden, the fruit trees, the barn with its flanking pine trees, the windmill — all slipped further and further away. The house and its contents — the beds, father's desk, the polished hardwood table in the parlor, the kitchen table and chairs, the kerosine stove, books and magazines on pine board shelves — were left as they were. The neighbor's cows again watched silently as the pickup went by.

Jo and his brother, Tak, sitting on the back of the pickup amid the rolled-up bedding and battered suitcases — you can take only what you can carry in your hands, they had been told — remained silent. The evacuation would be temporary, only for the duration of the war, the Army said. Looking at his brother, Jo remembered the words, "Ours but not ours." Would the farm remain theirs to come back to?

Jo tried to remember all the details of what he could see as the truck moved on. But it was his mother's face that brief moment before she got into the pickup that he remembered most — a face which seemed to be conveying something he had yet to understand.

Chapter Two
California *Nani-Yori*

March 21, 1942: The first advance groups of Japanese American "volunteers" arrive in Manzanar…(to) transform it into a "relocation center."

May 29, 1942: Largely organized by Quaker leader Clarence E. Pickett, the National Japanese-American Student Relocation Council is formed in Philadelphia with the University of Washington dean Robert W. O'Brien as director. By war's end 4,300 nisei would be in college.

○

Most of the dozen or so families that made up the congregation of the small Japanese-American church outside of Mountain View had gathered for the Easter service. The church attendance normally would have been smaller — they were farmers, and Easter the season for planting and tending early peas, green onions, carrots and radishes, or pruning orchards. But the evacuation was coming, and though everyone was busy getting ready for it, the families gathered for what they knew would be a farewell service. A few families had already gone east to avoid the incarceration. Sonoda-san, though he wasn't ordained, was conducting the service as he always did when the Japanese minister was not around and the parents were attending.

The strains of the last hymn had hardly died out — the parents sang in Japanese, their children in English — when Sonoda-san began his sermon for the day. He spoke in Japanese, but Jo could follow most of the words: "*Kami-sama*…God; *ai*…love, *gaman*…perseverance." It sounded like one of Sonoda-san's usual sermons.

He was in his late seventies, his hair white and wispy. He held his head erect, though his body, especially his shoulders, sagged with age. The old man's eye, however — his left one was gone by the time Jo's family had met him — sparkled as it darted first one way, then the other, seeking attention.

Jo was three years old when the family first moved into the area and had gone to the church for an initial visit. Sonoda-san, one of the founders of the church and often its unofficial greeter, picked Jo up. Jo remembered trying to squirm free when he noticed the man had only one eye. The man wore no eye patch, and though the eye lids had covered the hollow where the eye should have been, Jo stared at the spot — half scared, half fascinated.

Jo got used to the one eye and, for Jo, Sonoda-san became as much a part of the church as the wooden prism-shaped steeple, the white-washed outside walls, the brownish-yellow stained glass windows, the old wooden benches and their hymn racks, even the picture of Christ behind the lectern. Whenever Jo went to church, the old man was there. He'd pat Jo and the other children on their backs as they ran by, tousle their hair, or just give a friendly smile. Jo didn't pay much attention to all of this as a child, but as he grew older he realized that Sonoda-san, though he had a son and two grown daughters as well as grandchildren, also saw all the other children of the congregation as his own.

The drone of the old man's voice was starting to put Jo to sleep, when he realized the sermon was over and Sonoda-san was saying a last few words.

"*Mina-sama*...all of you will be leaving this area soon," he said, using polite, very formal Japanese. "I'm taking this opportunity to say '*Sayonara.*' Me — I'm an old man. This is my home. I want to be buried in California. Then they will not be able to move me."

Suddenly everyone woke up. What did he mean, wanting to be buried? Was he seriously ill? He couldn't be thinking suicide?

"California *nani-yori*...California is the most...," he started to say, but before he could finish his sentence, his voice broke and he began to cry. The right side of his face soon was drenched in tears. The left side, without an eye to give it full expression, remained dry.

For a minute or two the congregation remained frozen. The pre-teenage children were still, unsure of what to make of it all. Their older brothers and sisters, in their teens and early twenties, looked on, waited. The parents, however, though silent, were as one in their sympathy — through the corner of his eyes Jo could see his mother's face, a rare glistening of tears in her eyes.

Eventually, Sonoda-san's grown-up son, Roy, led his father off the stage, while some of the older people shook their heads and murmured, "*Kawaiso-ni*...poor man."

Jo stood up in his seat next to the aisle as Sonoda-san was being led by. He wanted to put his arm on the old man's shoulder, lend some support. Instead, Sonoda-san reached out first. The old man said nothing, but his firm grip on Jo's shoulder let Jo know his sympathy was appreciated.

Jo didn't see Sonoda-san or his family again until Santa Anita.

"Please go see who's on the train," his mother had asked. The rumors were that this would be the last train in from the San Francisco Bay area and many of the family friends had not arrived yet.

Jo stood about 30 yards away from the railway siding where the train had pulled in. The MP's had roped off the area next to the platform where the baggage was being collected and checked, and the people registered. Standing on a rise on the ground, he could look over the crowd and at the anxious faces looking out from the train windows. He recognized a face here and there, but didn't bother to wave; they probably would not have seen him anyway. He could remember when he and his family had come just a week before. Several hundred people were standing by the siding and from the train, all that could be seen was a mass of faces darkened by the hot southern California sun, staring in, not individuals.

He didn't see the Sonoda's until they were already off the train and through the registration line, gathering their baggage for loading onto waiting trucks.

After short greetings — Roy, his wife Ayako, and his sister Edith, all looking worn from the train ride — Jo looked for the rest of the family. The older sister, Jo was told, had gone to Tanforan with her husband and children. He was about to ask, when he saw Sonoda-san standing off to the side.

"Sonoda-san...," Jo started to say as he turned when Roy gently grabbed his shoulder and forewarned, "He might not respond."

Sonoda-san was standing there, staring into the distance with his one good eye. He wore a black eye patch, something Jo saw him do in the past only on formal occasions such as a wedding or a funeral. He seemed oblivious to things around him and gave just a slight nod when he saw Jo.

Some weeks passed before Jo saw Sonoda-san again, though Jo's parents had visited the old man several times. Jo had gone to a judo class and was walking along the east fence to the camp when he saw Ayako sitting with her father-in-law in the shade of a guard tower.

"Might as well take advantage of what we have," she said with a smile when Jo noted the source of the shade. "How've you been?"

"Okay," Jo said, then turning to Sonoda-san, asked, "*Ikaga desuka?*"

"*Ma...,*" the old man responded.

"How's he been feeling?" Jo asked Ayako.

"Seems a bit better now," she said. "He enjoys visitors; your parents, for instance. I wish he would relax more, enjoy the rest he's getting like the other old folks are."

"He should," Jo said, "He, they, deserve it."

After a little while, Ayako said, "If you're not in a hurry I have a favor to ask."

"Got lots of time."

"Would you sit with my father while I go to the post office? I don't like to leave him alone."

"Sure."

After Ayako left, Jo and the old man sat silently watching the scene. Only about a hundred yards away, on the other side of the fence, cars whizzed by on the asphalt highway. Across the highway they could see the bright yellow sign of a Shell gas station, a Miller's hardware, and a Rexall drug store, all on the main street of the small town of Arcadia. A larger building, whose front was not visible, was probably the town's movie house. To the right, and a bit in the distance, a green and black electric train going from Pasadena to Los Angeles seemed almost noiseless as it went by.

As he watched the train through the simmering heat waves, it occurred to Jo that in the 15 or so years since his family joined the church and he had known Sonoda-san, he had never sat and had a real conversation with him.

"*Ojii-san*, how are you feeling?" Jo finally asked.

"*Genki-dessho* -- fine, I suppose," he said. He paused, then said, "Ayako *shimpai* worries about me. She shouldn't. I don't feel like saying too much now days, that's all."

"That's okay," Jo said. He could see the light brown blotches of age on the old man's cheeks and forehead. Stubby white whiskers matched the color of his wispy hair. What Jo wanted to see, however, was some of the sparkle that used to show in the old man's eye.

They did not talk much more before Ayako returned. Two days later Jo stopped by again, sat and talked a little with Ayako. Sonoda-san nodded when Jo arrived, but again said little. After that day, Jo stopped by regularly after his judo class. Since Roy was working in the administrative office and Edith teaching in the makeshift school set up in the racetrack grandstand, neither was home during midday, so Jo's visits gave Ayako a chance to do her errands or get over to the canteen.

Little by little, Sonoda-san began to talk as he and Jo sat. Noticing Jo's *judo-gi* one day, he smiled a bit, then said, "Used to take judo myself. Became a *san-dan* — a third level black belt."

"You must have been good," Jo said. His instructors were of the same rank.

"Well," the old man said, then conceded, "I could have been. Life seemed so simple then." He paused, reminisced. "We were farm boys, were taught that hard work always produced just rewards. We were young."

On another occasion he talked of being a *hei-tai* — a soldier — during the first Sino-Japanese War. He said a person had to have been in Japan then to sense the nationalistic atmosphere of the time. "People talked of '*Dai Nippon*' — Greater Japan — and 'Japan's Destiny.' They, I, believed it all, then," he said. He said he volunteered for the Army like almost all of the other youths in his village, that he felt lucky when he was accepted, luckier still when he got his orders to go to China.

Once in China, though — they landed in Tsingtao — things were quite different, he said. All they did was walk, walk, walk. His unit did not see any real battle, just minor skirmishes. What he remembered most were the refugees — kids, women, old men — clogging the roads, fleeing with nowhere to go.

"But your eye?" Jo asked.

"That came much later," Sonoda-san said, laughing softly. "Happened while I was pruning my orchard — a branch fell freakishly. In China I didn't even get a scratch."

He said he lost something else in China — his patriotic zeal and the so-called "*Bushido* Spirit" — the "way of the warrior."

He returned to Japan disillusioned; became restless, dissatisfied, finally turned to Christianity. Christianity is what made him turn toward America, he said. He did a lot of reading — about the American revolution, the Constitution and its Bill of Rights, religious freedom, the pursuit of happiness, a wide open land. America gave him something to believe in again, he said.

Here, he paused, seemed to be thinking to himself.

"I had absolutely nothing when I came," he said. "In Japan I didn't even have anything to sell, only had a small bank account, had to borrow from my parents to get enough for my passage, but I had to see America. For me it was hope."

San Francisco — *So-ko* — he called it, was not what he wanted. He lived in *Nihon-machi* — Japanese town — stayed in a Japanese hotel, ate Japanese food. It was almost like being back in Japan. Besides, the only job he could find was washing dishes, again in a Japanese restaurant.

But America offered change, he said. He had heard that they needed laborers to shovel salt from the drying beds lining San Francisco Bay off of the 101 Highway near Mayfield. It was hard work. He said the salt was a couple of inches thick, heavy, had to be broken up in cakes, then shoveled onto wheel barrows holding several hundred pounds. He said he ate two, even three times as much as normal to get the energy and strength needed for the work. But it gave him weekends off to look for something more permanent.

"*Kusa darake* — nothing but weeds" they said when he first went to investigate an old farm he had been told about. Too many rocks. The soil's too poor. It's too close to the Bay. He said everyone he had asked gave him reasons why the land could no longer be farmed.

But he could see the weeds growing. Obviously other plants could grow as well, he was sure. People were maybe just afraid of the hard work it would take to make the land productive. No farmer in Japan would let land go to waste that way, he said. and no matter how he looked at it he would never have been able to own anything in his village in Japan that would even approach his farm in California.

Sometimes he wondered whether his walnut orchard was being irrigated properly, whether anyone would bother to spray his persimmon tree, a rare variety he grew from a seed sent over from Japan, or whether anyone knew how to properly trim his *bonsai*. His Italian neighbors, the Parodi's, said they would look after things, but they were dairy farmers and knew little about caring for orchards or delicate plants.

If he had any regrets, he said, it was that he did not come to America sooner.

"*Kiyoiku* — education. I missed my chance," he said. If he had not gotten married, been so busy, he might even have gone back to school, even at a late age.

"But it's you younger people I worry about now," he said. "Who knows how long the war is going to go on, or how long they'll keep us in these camps. They can't, they mustn't keep you people out of school too long. Your future...they'll destroy everything the older generation is striving for."

It was mid-July. More than two months had passed since the last families had been moved into Santa Anita. People in the camp were getting restless. When was something going to happen? Where were they going to end up? Rumors were all that people had to go by.

Jo could notice the effect of the uncertainty even on his parents and the other Issei, most of whom said little about being interned. Outwardly, at least, they seemed better able to cope with things than their offsprings.

"All these rumors, do you know anything that's true?" Sonoda-san asked when Jo made his usual visit.

"They've always said that Santa Anita was only a temporary camp," Jo said, "so I'm sure they'll move us inland. But where and when, I don't know."

"I don't care much any more if they do or don't move me out of California," Sonoda-san said. "It's just that..."

A slight twitch in the old man's face indicated that hurt was still there.

"It's still you younger people I worry about," Sonoda-san continued. "Anything happening with you?"

"Not really," Jo said, "but they're talking about getting college students back into school."

"Not just a rumor?"

"I don't think so," Jo said. "Haven't talked to her directly, but I've heard that the Ishimoto girl, Mary, was getting a grant to continue her education at Radcliffe."

"Radcliffe? The women's college connected with Harvard?" Sonoda-san asked.

"*Eh...*," he said, mouth open in surprise when Jo nodded. "Imagine, Ishimoto-san's daughter going to Radcliffe. It seems so exclusive. We're all nothing but poor dirt farmers. I knew she was smart, but... Will others be getting a chance too?"

"Probably," Jo said.

"Jo, you don't know what you started," Ayako said a few days later.

"Oh?"

"This thing about Mary and Radcliffe. He wouldn't give me any peace until I went and asked Mary myself. Mary said it's been confirmed. She's just received notice of a fellowship, will be leaving soon."

"Great," Jo said.

"Wait. That's not all. Father's changed. I don't know whether it's this thing about Mary, or maybe because it seems like we'll know soon which camps people will be slated for. Anyway Mary and the school thing definitely helped. He keeps mumbling about renewed..."

"Jo, have you heard?" Sonoda-san said, interrupting as he came out of the barracksstruggling with a large atlas. "They say we're going to Wyoming." His eye lit up as he talked.

"They say the camp will be near Cody, just south of Yellowstone," the old man continued. "Maybe we'll be surrounded by nothing but sage brush, who knows. But look, the map shows mountains; it's cattle country."

Jo looked as Sonoda-san sat, holding a magnifying glass over the open atlas on his lap.

"Nothing's all that definite yet," Jo cautioned. But as he peered over the old man's shoulder, he could almost physically feel the man's enthusiasm.

"He's acting like a ten-year-old," Ayako said with a laugh. "He's been asking, even as he's looking at the map: 'Where's this place? How many miles from the West Coast? How high up?' I don't know what to think of him at times."

"*Shinpai-nai* — not to worry," the old man responded, then turning back to Jo, said, "Did you know? Cody is up about 5,000 feet. Imagine. I've never been out of California since I arrived; must have been almost 40 years ago. Now maybe I'll be able *to…*" Sonoda-san's face was alive; his eye darted over the page. He also wore his eye patch. He was ready to travel.

Two days later when Jo walked in from the sunlight into the stable where his family was housed, he knew something was wrong. Even as his eyes were adjusting to the dimmer light, they caught the glimmer of silk. His mother was wearing her good dress and Sunday hat, though it wasn't Sunday. His father, in a dark suit, stood quietly by.

"*Chotto,*" his mother beckoned. "*Sonoda-san ga nakunari-mashita,*" she said simply. They were going to his memorial service.

"But I saw him only the day before yesterday," Jo protested. " How? Why?"

"A stroke, something like that," his father said. "*Toshi* — his age. No one expected it."

Jo watched from the open upper half of the swinging stable door as his mother and father walked out into the hot sun and down the road between the row of stables toward the tar-papered barracks where a temporary chapel had been set up in one of them. His parents showed no tears though his mother's steps were slow, weary.

"California *nani-yori* …," the old man had said. California is the most… what? Jo wanted to ask.

Moving back into the stable, Jo lay back on his cot, studying the underside of the boards of the roof. Some of the whitewash had fallen off; bits of cobweb hung between supporting two-by-fours. The smell of the lime used to smother the odor of the stable permeated the air; the stale straw in his canvas mattress bag stunk. His gaze moved from the roof to the plywood separating his stable from the next where a triangular gap allowed in even the softest sounds.

"*Nen-ne, nen-ne*," he could hear a mother in the next stable whispering as a low whimper was replaced by the sound of a baby suckling.

Armed Guards by by Chizuko Judy Sugita de Queiroz. From her book *Camp Days: 1942-1945*.

Chapter Three:
A Sunday In Santa Anita

Feb. 2, 1942: "*A viper is nonetheless a viper wherever the egg is hatched....* *So, as a Japanese American born of Japanese parents, nurtured upon Japanese traditions, living in a transplanted Japanese atmosphere and thoroughly inoculated with Japanese...ideals, notwithstanding his nominal brand of accidental citizenship almost inevitably and with the rarest exceptions grows up to be a Japanese, and not an American in his ... ideas, and is...menacing...unless...hamstrung.*" Los Angeles Times editorial.

Aug. 4, 1942: A routine search for contraband at the Santa Anita "Assembly Center" turns into a "riot." Eager military personnel became overzealous and abusive, which, along with the failure of several attempts to reach the camp's internal security chief, triggered mass unrest, crowd formations and harassment of the searchers. Military police with tanks and machine guns quickly ended the incident. Commission 82

O

"Are they prisoners of war or what, Sir?" the soldier asked.

The lieutenant looked at the questioner, then toward the window. Outside he could see the sentry post, and the black and white-striped cross bars at the main gate. The fresh lumber of a newly erected guard tower gleamed in the sun. Behind the barbed wire fence, were the rows of horse stables and the parking lot where temporary barracks had been set up.

"I don't know if they're considered PW's," the lieutenant finally said. He looked down at the mimeograph sheets on the lectern in front of him. "These papers don't tell me. They're internees, but mostly U.S. citizens, I suppose."

"Hell. They're just a bunch of Japs," a voice said. Others, feeling more at ease, laughed.

"We're at Santa Anita. Where are the race horses?" someone else asked.

The lieutenant put up his hands, enough was enough. "All right. Settle down. We're here on serious business. Here are your general orders:

"One — no, I stress 'no' talking to the internees unless on official business.

Two — nobody goes in or out of the camp except through the front post. The post, guard towers and the guard posts are marked on the map on the rear wall..."

Geordie, sitting two-thirds of the way back in the rows of school-room chairs with writing arms, listened with half an ear. He wanted to get back to his bunk and write home to his sister Molly to let the family know he was still in California. Two weeks ago he had been on leave after finishing basic training and a short M.P. course at Fort Ord. His orders said to report to the Army replacement depot at Camp Stoneman. That usually meant sure shipment to somewhere in the Pacific.

When they started getting their gear to ship out, though, he knew he and the others of the platoon might not be going to the Pacific after all. They got the old Springfield rifle instead of the new Garand M-1. They got fatigues, field jackets, combat boots and steel helmets, but the steel helmets were World War I types, and they were issued two sets of Khakis and low cut shoes.

"Sir, may I ...?" Pvt. Barkley started to ask as the lieutenant turned over the last of the mimeographed sheets.

Goddam ass, why doesn't he shut up, Geordie thought. Geordie first met Barkley in basic training, got stuck with the guy at the M.P. school. Now here he was, stuck with the guy again.

"Barkley's the name," the guy had said when they first met. "From Sequoia; you?"

None of your fucking business, Geordie was tempted to say. The guy's approach bothered him — a faked air of confidence, maybe arrogance. Geordie just looked at the guy — about six feet, blond, skin too fair, a city type.

"Geordie. Geordie Jepson," he finally said. "From Santa Clara. Oklahoma originally."

"Oh, an Okie," Barkley said. He was about to say more, than stopped when he saw Geordie's look.

Geordie never liked the guy from then on. But before the week was to be over everyone in the training battalion seemed to have heard about the Barkleys from Sequoia — mainly from Barkley.

Geordie was surprised the morning after the briefing when, at roll call, he heard the sergeant say that the uniform of the day was full battle gear

— steel helmets, combat boots, fatigues, field jackets, web belting, rifles, bayonets.

"There's another trainload coming in," the sergeant said. "Several hundred."

"Why all the gear?" one of the new soldiers asked.

"Just follow orders, okay?"

"Where's the train coming from?" another soldier asked.

"San Jose, Santa Clara, other places just south of 'Frisco from what I've heard. Don't matter where, just keep on your toes."

San Jose? Santa Clara? Geordie had graduated from Santa Clara Union High School just two years before. He wondered — maybe he would he see Jo or some of the others he knew? Tak, Kenji, Mas, Shizuko — outside of Jo, Geordie couldn't remember the last names, but they were classmates.

Since graduating high school Geordie often would wonder what happened to Jo, who was a year behind Geordie at school, in Molly's class. He and Jo were teammates on the high school wrestling team. They didn't talk that often, but there was a bond — both went out for wrestling because the team practiced during school hours, not after school as with most sports. Both had to be home from school as soon as possible to help out at home — Jo, because he lived on a farm; Geordie, so he'd be available whenever odd jobs came his family's way.

Geordie's family lived in a trailer camp then — on the 101 Highway near Cupertino; had lived there almost two years. For those summers, Molly and his mother picked raspberries on the nearby Sugamo farm. The trailer camp was no better nor no worse than the others the family had lived in, but at the time the family was out of money, had no work. School had already started.

Things were bad for almost everyone they knew. Because of price or labor disputes, the newspapers regularly had pictures of fruit of all kinds (including oranges that he loved), tomatoes, even milk in Wisconsin being dumped into roadside ditches. He often didn't know what the issues were — only that he, his family and his friends were hungry while all that good food was being dumped to rot in the sun.

Molly came home with the news. Jo told her in class that his father told him to tell her that she and her family should pick what lettuce they could from the patch on the Sugamo farm. The price of lettuce in the wholesale market in San Francisco was down to 50 cents a crate, not enough to pay for the cost of the wooden crates and having the produce trucked to the market.

"Not worth the picking," is what Jo said, and his father had decided to have the patch plowed under; maybe the Jepson family would like some.

It was not so much the lettuce. Until then Geordie had felt that no one in California cared or even had the least concern for the welfare of people from the dust bowl; only that they wanted the "Okies" and "Arkies" to go elsewhere.

Geordie forced himself to keep his eyes straight ahead, soldier-like, as the squad marched through the front gate, passed the stable area housing some of the internees, and to the railway siding where the newcomers were processed. But out of the corner of his eyes he could see blankets and clothes on lines strung in front of some of the stables; children of all sizes, openly curious and watching; the adults, also curious but watching with side glances. The conditions were squalid, but maybe no worse than the trailer camps.

A crowd had already gathered below the loading platform as the second squad marched up and came to parade rest behind the registration desk. The crowd stirred as the train pulled in. At first there was a wave here and there, smiles as onlookers recognized people on the train.

Unemotional; the Japanese never show their true feelings, Geordie had read. But then as he watched, he noticed a teenage girl — 15 or 16 years old in Levis, white cotton blouse, red canvas sun hat — waving excitedly at a small group clustered near a window of the train. As those of the group returned her wave, the girl smiled broadly. Suddenly, however, she dropped her arms and burst into tears. Her family? A boy friend's? Relatives? Geordie then noticed other women crying; even some of the men wiping their eyes.

The major in charge of the detail watched over the registration of the new arrivals while his two aides — a captain and a first lieutenant — checked the blanket rolls, the duffle bags, assorted suitcases and other baggage for contraband.

Geordie, in the front row of the squad, searched their faces. He'd give a signal of some kind if he saw anyone he knew. An old couple — maybe in their seventies, the old man in a drab dark suit, the woman in a black silk dress with a 1920-style hat — stood in front of him for a while, anxiety and puzzlement written on their faces. They held hands, as kindergarten children do going in and out of their classroom, while they waited.

He then noticed a little girl — soft round face, black hair tumbling over her shoulders from under a white bonnet, a pink and yellow bib —

still on the train, gazing patiently out of the window as others around her gathered their belongings from overhead racks. When she turned, her eyes and Geordie's met for a moment, maybe several seconds, until Geordie pulled his eyes away. He looked down, then to his right and left at the squad, wondered why the bayonets. When he looked up again, the little girl was gone.

Geordie was not paying much attention to the captain and the lieutenant as they checked the baggage. The captain, in spite of his white leather gloves, still used a swagger stick when checking women's suitcases, using the stick to gingerly move aside slips, panties, hose and other such clothing. When he heard the captain cough, Geordie looked up. Everyone else was also watching.

The captain had found something. His red mustached face was full of expectancy as he raised to eye level some bundled up silk underwear, apparently wrapped around a tissue-covered package. The open suitcase in front of him belonged to a family of three — a middle-aged man in a farmer's new blue denim overalls; his wife, her hair in a bun highlighting a ruddy face, and a daughter, probably in her early twenties, a bit overdressed in a print dress and a fancy straw hat.

With the swagger stick tucked under his elbow, the captain began unwrapping the small bundle. The daughter gasped at the glint of glass. The bottle then slipped. The captain tried to catch it, but it slipped through his gloved hands and shattered on the ground.

Geordie could see three faces simultaneously — the captain's, lit up as if to say: Aha, caught you; the daughter's, red with embarrassment and humiliation; the father's, chagrin

showing through a silly grin.

"*Naze? Son nani...*" the daughter began scolding her father, then stopped, bringing her hands up to hide her face. The father, his hands in his pockets, looked down at the shattered bottle. Then, stepping around the broken glass, moved to close up the baggage which had already been checked. The smell of the bourbon still permeated the air as the man, a duffle bag in one hand and bundled bedding in the other, moved defiantly to a waiting truck. The daughter, carrying the suitcase, avoided everyone's eyes as she followed. The mother gave the captain a slight bow before picking up a carrier bag and hurrying to catch up to the other two.

Geordie knew good whiskey and the need sometimes for a good stiff drink.

Geordie stood against the wooden railing at the top of Guard Post 5, looking out into the darkness while Barkley manned the searchlight. Throughout the camp proper, 25-watt bulbs, placed every 50 yards or so, were like little pinpricks in the darkness, stretching from the nearby stable area to the far end of the camp a mile away. Only an occasional light could be seen in the nearby town of Arcadia. The only real light came from the searchlights on each of the two dozen guard towers surrounding the camp. The beams formed kaleidoscopic patterns as they lengthened and shortened as they crisscrossed with each sweep of the fence areas.

The quiet gave Geordie time to think about the families in the camp, about his own family. His father now worked full time at the Hendy Ironworks in Sunnyvale — defense contracts, big expansion. "But I can't even tell you, a soldier, what I do," he had said several times with an air of importance during Geordie's home leave. "Defense secrets, you know."

Molly and his mother had planned to work the summer in Libby's cannery, but his dad said Hendy might hire them first. Jeff, his younger brother, was being recruited to work in the orchards even before his high school was out for summer vacation. The family, with the added income, finally was buying a house.

But the faces of the people at the unloading platform — the teenage girl, the old couple, the baby girl in the train window, the man with the whiskey — made him feel again the hopelessness he felt when his family had to leave Oklahoma. His big worry then, as they loaded beds, tables, chairs, suitcases, clothes, everything they owned onto the old truck, was whether the truck would ever make it to California. It got to California all right, but — they were told by a fat sheriff in the middle of the night to pack up and move; they had to fight for space in a dirty trailer camp; they picked peaches for eight or ten hours a day for a couple of dollars. His mother often cried when she wondered out loud if getting to California was really worth it.

"Hey, you see the newspaper today?" Barkley asked, breaking the silence. "Paper said they've found proof that some of these Japs, before we rounded them up, were trying to signal a submarine of the coast not too far from here. It's like what they did in Hawaii, cut swathes in cane fields pointing toward Pearl Harbor. They can't be trusted."

"I don't know about that," Geordie said.

"Hell yes," Barkley said. "Some of them don't even speak English. They might even try to pull something right in this camp. Wouldn't surprise me one bit."

Geordie said nothing. In the darkness he could not make out Barkley's face; the voice, though, indicated Barkley believed it all.

The sun was up high and the barracks were getting warm. Geordie lay on his bunk; he'd have to decide soon — it would be too hot to stay inside. Go into L.A., see a movie? Maybe even stay in town for the night. Might be kind of nice, he was thinking, when he heard voices raised at the far end of the barracks.

"All passes canceled? Bull shit," someone said. "Damn, don't kid us."

"I'm not. They're rioting. It's an emergency," a corporal wearing an M.P. helmet liner, gold braid and a black M.P. armband, shouted back. "All of you already dressed, come with me right now."

The original briefing officer, now wearing the white hat of an M.P., then stuck his head in the doorway as several of the men snapped to attention.

"Corporal's right," was all he said, then moved on.

In the confusion Geordie did not get full details, though he sensed the tension. In minutes, he was dressed. Then he sat like the others, waiting for further orders.

"See. What'd I tell you the other night," Barkley, sitting on his footlocker across the aisle, said. "Christ, they may have even planned this."

"What crap," Slim, sitting several bunks away, countered. "Guy from the other platoon said the trouble started because they began searching the stable area for contraband — hot plates, flat irons, stuff like that."

"How's the guy know?" Barkley shot back. "He..."

A news bulletin was just getting started on a small radio on the wall when the orders were shouted to fall out. "Twenty-two thousand Japs, in a major uprising at the detention center at the Santa Anita race track, are..." was all Geordie caught of the bulletin.

The morning had started out so peacefully. The sun was out, but she felt a cool breeze. Maybe it would not become too hot. The two, with baby held between them, had walked at the baby's pace to the mess hall. Since it was Sunday, people slept late and the mess hall was quiet with just a few people. In the back of her mind, she remembered the notice — some kind of inspection was scheduled. But it seemed unimportant; the day was so nice.

After breakfast, on their way back to the stable area, they saw a crowd of people lined up on both sides of the broad street leading into the camp from the front gate. Soldiers, about 50 of them, had marched in and were standing in formation in the middle of the asphalt.

"I wonder what's happening," she said, instinctively picking up her daughter as her husband went to ask.

"It's nothing," her husband said as he returned. "It's that dumb inspection; people are upset by it. Now, maybe they'll have enough sense to stop it."

What he said seemed true. Even as they watched, the soldiers shouldered their rifles, did an about face, and marched back to the front gate, only about 100 yards away.

Back at the stables, people stood in groups. Mrs. Hatano and Mrs. Honda, from the Bay area, turned from their conversation to bow greetings as she and her husband walked by. She was quite proud of her husband. He was maintaining such a good front. When they first arrived in Santa Anita and saw the stables, he laughed and said, "Hell, when I first came to America I had to live in an old box car a farmer had plunked in the middle of his fields. This is nothing. It'll teach some of these youngsters; show them how the old timers had to do it."

He also stopped talking about exceptions being made. For a while he had been convinced that he, she and the baby would be exempt from the evacuation order. He had been to an American Legion convention in Sacramento only a few months before Pearl Harbor. He met Governor Olson and Attorney General Warren. "Even had a chance to give them my card," he told her later. "Hell, I'm a World War I veteran. They won't let it happen to us."

For a full week after the evacuation notices were put up at the post offices, on telephone poles, and on storefronts in Gardena, he scanned the local and Los Angeles newspapers carefully. When he could find nothing about exceptions being made, he shrugged. "They're too busy with mobilization. They'll get around to it later," he had been convinced. But that was months ago. He got no reply to several letters he had sent off and now seemed to have accepted the fact that he, she and the baby would have to be in camp like all the others.

About noon, when it was time to go to the nursery station to get the baby's formula, she thought about skipping lunch. The station was in the opposite direction from the mess hall. Rather than all that walking, they could buy some snacks at the canteen instead of returning to the mess hall.

She was about to ask her husband what he wanted to do, when she heard the grinding of motors.

"What's happening, Henry?" she asked her husband who was playing with the baby in his arms.

"Sounds like trucks or something. Let me go see," he said, stepping outside the stable, the baby still in his arms.

Moments later, as the sound of the motors became louder, she went to look out of the open upper half of the stable door. To her surprise, she saw a truck, machine gun mounted, followed by an armored half-track carrying a half dozen helmeted soldiers with bayoneted rifles between their knees. The huge white stars painted on the sides of the truck and the half-track gleamed in the sun. Then, suddenly, she heard her husband's voice above the sound of the motors.

"The asses, the Goddam asses," she could hear him shout to two of the neighbors' teenaged sons. "Who and what the hell do they think we are? Women and children are here. What are those carriers and machine guns for? Damn it, we don't even have any rocks to throw."

She caught a glimpse of her husband's face — jaws set tight, eyes glaring despite the baby squirming in his arms. Suddenly she was afraid; not for herself, not for baby. She was so afraid her husband's hurt would show.

○

"Ever handle one of these things before?" the Captain asked, pointing to the machine gun mounted on the turret of the truck. "It's a 50-calibre."

"Fired it once in basic, Sir," Geordie replied.

"Good. She's all yours, then," the Captain said. "Also, you men from the M.P. unit here know the camp better then my men. You act as guide on this truck. You're to patrol Section B of the stable area. No stopping. Just go up and down in front of the rows of stables."

By the time the truck reached the stable area, people were streaming back from the grandstand area, where a crowd had gathered in front of the administrative offices there seeking information. Some kids were running about, but Geordie saw no real signs of disorder. Most of the people even stayed on the walking paths, careful not to step on the flower beds along side. "A major uprising," the radio had said.

"There are four rows of stables here, six more further up. We can start at this edge," Geordie instructed the driver. With the inspection that had started the demonstration already called off, the situation was calm. Geordie half expected the trucks and half-tracks to be called back to the motor pool. But he heard the major say over the walkie-talkie that "We got to show 'em," and the patrolling continued.

As the truck moved down the unpaved street between the low, white-washed stables, the people moved aside, some deliberately slow. Geordie, leaning against the metal turret of the machine gun, could feel the eyes focussed his way because of the weapon. Just beyond the hedges separating Section B from Section A of the stable area, he saw the truck there come into view. On it he could see Barkley in the turret position, his hands on the machine gun as if he was ready to shoot on moments notice.

Geordie's truck swung around a corner and was starting up the next street, when suddenly he saw a little girl. He was sure it was the same girl he had seen a few weeks before in the train window. She was wearing a tiny straw hat instead of her bonnet and was being carried in the arms of a man in a white T-shirt.

She recognized Geordie, made him smile. The little girl then shyly started to raise her hand for a friendly wave when the man's hand went up and cut the wave short. Geordie's smile became a distorted grin. He then shifted his eyes to the man's face — broad, well-tanned under neatly trimmed bushy black hair. The flush of anger Geordie felt when the little girl's wave was cut off, stopped. The man was crying.

As Geordie started turning away, he suddenly noticed the person standing next to the man. The posture, the body build — he knew who it was before he even looked into the sunburned face. "Jo," he wanted to shout.

The truck was moving. A wink or a nod would not have been noticed. Geordie waved. Jo, his hands stuck in the back pockets of his Levi's, looked up. Geordie was sure Jo saw his face. But there was no sign of recognition. The look Geordie saw on his friend's face was the same look he used to see on Jo's face at the start of a wrestling match, one which masked all feelings.

Chapter Four
Rape In A Whorehouse

July 6, 1943: "This time the WRA decided to fight back... Testimony of WRA head Dillon Myer and others in Washington, D.C. ... thoroughly discredit earlier witnesses who...(made) sensational statements based on half-truths, exaggerations, and falsehoods." (In testimony before a subcommittee of the Dies Committee on Un-American Activities; Commission report, page 226-227)

O

Dayton, a small town in southeastern Washington State, was beautiful in the spring and summer of 1943 — rolling green hills of young wheat backed by high, pine-covered mountains; clear streams; and a main street nestled at the of a vale by the Touchet River, which had full spring salmon runs.

It could have been a town that Jo may have gotten to like. But during the four months he spent in the area — he cut asparagus and later harvested peas for the Blue Mountain Canneries — he hardly met any of the town's people outside of Jim, the foreman, and Bill, his assistant, who drove around from one field to another to check on the work crews.

Jo and his friend Fuzzy were among 100 or so workers recruited from the wartime "relocation centers" in Heart Mountain, Wyoming, and Minidoka, Idaho, where Americans of Japanese descent and their parents were interned during World War II. In Dayton, the workers were housed in barrack-like bunkhouses in a compound on the edge of town across from a main highway. Though he never spoke to any to find out, the attitude of the townspeople seemed to be that the workers — "the Japs" — could be tolerated as long as they worked the fields and bought goods from the stores in town, but otherwise kept to themselves.

Jo's attitude was the hell with them, too. He'd work their fields — he got paid 75 cents an hour versus the $12 a month he got paid for shoveling coal from box cars in the camp at Heart

Mountain. He didn't want to meet them anymore than they wanted to meet him. The town needed the workers if the peas were to be harvested; they'd have to put up with him and the others whether they liked it or not.

Fuzzy — his and Jo's family were neighbors since the two were in grade school — probably would have liked to have met some of the townspeople. After all, it was his idea in the first place that he and Jo sign up for the work with the cannery. "Might as well use the opportunity to see some of the country, get to know other people," Fuzzy had said. But, of course, Fuzzy didn't get to meet any more people than any of the other workers.

What seemed a silent confrontation between the townspeople and the workers lasted through the spring and summer. Then things came to a head suddenly, on a Sunday.

The pea harvest was at its peak. In the cannery itself, which flew the "E" for efficiency banner, the townspeople — women, teenagers, men too old for the draft, others waiting to be drafted — worked three shifts. Out in the fields the peas were cut, vines and all, by machine, then hauled to viners which culled the vines and the pods from the peas. The workers from the relocation centers worked two shifts, from 4 a.m. to 2 p.m., and from 4 p.m. to 2 a.m. Speedy harvest was essential. Once the peas had matured, they had to be harvested in a day or two, or they'd become over-ripe, hard, and no longer sweet. Jo and Fuzzy worked the late shift.

That Sunday, Jo would have slept a bit longer, but since it was the only day of the week off, and though there was no where to go, he didn't want to waste time sleeping and was awake by 9 a.m. It was already hot, and he decided to take a shower before planning the rest of his day.

He stepped out of his bunkhouse in his jeans and slippers, bare above the waist except for a towel over his shoulders, then stopped short. A police car was parked in the center of the lawn which covered the square formed by bunkhouses on three sides and a mess hall and shower area on the fourth. Two uniformed policemen sat in the front seat of the car with shotguns held purposely so that they could be seen through the car windows.

Now what? he was thinking, then saw two other police cars and the two-toned tan and brown coupe of Jim, the foreman. These cars were parked by the gate to the wire mesh fence surrounding the entire compound. Jim, a head taller than the workers around him, a shorter man in a gray, light cotton suit, and several uniformed policemen, all fat and tall, were talking to about 30 of the workers grouped in a semi-circle around the front of the cars. Most of the workers were half-dressed like Jo.

"What's up?" Jo asked when he saw Fuzzy standing on the edge of the group.

"Hell, I don't know," Fuzzy said, a frown on his usually grinning face. "Supposed to have been a rape in town."

"So?"

"Woman claims it was someone from here."

"One of us?" Jo asked.

"Yeah. Meantime they say we're not to leave this compound. Not to go downtown."

"They arresting us all or something?"

Fuzzy shrugged.

Up front the anger and agitation heightened. "We're not damn PWs the way you seem to think," Blackie, one of the older workers, almost shouted in the face of the light-suited man.

"We're still investigating the woman's complaint," the man said. "Meanwhile, the police ..."

"Balls." Blackie's voice became louder.

The man in the light suit, later identified as a "Mr. Brody," the town's deputy mayor, stepped back. The policemen shuffled, ready to move.

"We won't work," someone next to Blackie shouted.

"Yeah, we'll strike," another said.

In the commotion, Jim, the foreman, his tropical hat now askew, held up his hands and shouted, "Wait. Wait. Blackie, you others ... please. Let's not be hasty." Jim's job was to make sure the peas were harvested in time.

"Hell, if we weren't kicked out of California, we'd be harvesting our own peas," Blackie said.

There was further shouting, but the foreman finally prevailed. The policemen had the shotguns.

It was agreed that no moves would be made until after a meeting the next day of all the workers in the mess hall. The deputy mayor also agreed that the policemen, except for two in one car at the gate, would leave while the investigation of the rape charge continued. In the meantime, the workers would remain in the compound and stay out of town.

It took no organizing; no one had to present a case. But most of the workers were adamant. None of the crews would go to work as long as the town remained off limits. Of course, some remained reluctant. Each worker could earn a couple of hundred dollars in the weeks left before the end of the harvest. They wanted the money; some needed it badly. Others had other reasons.

"Why fuck up," Takeda, who ran card and crap games in Jo's bunkhouse, said. "I like it here." Takeda didn't even look up as he spoke, but kept his eyes focused on the cards he was dealing and the faces of the five players seated around the blanket-covered card table.

"Yeah," his friend Nakano said, "no fuck up." Nakano, seated nearby on a bottom bunk, had a half-pint whiskey bottle in his hand. In Minidoka, he said, he could not get even a beer, and that, he said, was hell.

Takeda and Nakano were both from Seattle, where Takeda ran a "club" with Nakano a lesser partner. Takeda — short, slim, thinning black hair always slicked straight back — had set up his card table in the bunkhouse the first night after the work crews arrived. Since then, five or six regulars and a handful of occasional players sought their luck nightly at blackjack, poker, or "*shi-go-ro*," a three-dice crap game. It was easy to tell who had won or lost after a night's gambling — the winners went to bed, the losers went out to work when their shift started.

Rumors about what was happening because of the threatened strike spread through the rest of the morning and into the afternoon. A train already was standing by in the railway yard in Pasco, 50 or so miles to the west of Dayton, ready to take the workers back to the camps in Idaho and Wyoming if they were not back in the fields by Tuesday, one report claimed. The local radio stations in Dayton, Pasco and Walla Walla were said to be asking that all able-bodied people prepare for forming emergency work crews. Newsmen from as far away as Spokane were said to be in town to cover the story. The head of the War Relocation Authority office in Denver was said to be flying in for the workers' meeting Monday.

Jo, only recently turned 18, kept telling himself it was no big deal. "So what if we're sent back to Wyoming," he said to Fuzzy. "We'd have a place to sleep. We'd be able to eat. We wouldn't even have to work if we didn't want to."

"Yeah, but...," Fuzzy said. Nobody was that anxious to return to the camps.

By mid afternoon, in spite of the rumors, activity in the compound slowed to the more normal Sunday routine. The laundermat next to the mess hall was busy; several workers sat in the shade of a bunkhouse waiting their turns for a haircut from Hirata, whose makeshift barber shop included a high stool for customers to sit on and an empty apple box to lay his clippers, scissors and combs on. Other workers were lolling around the bunkhouses or in the shade of small elm trees on the edge of the center lawn; some were reading, others writing letters.

Nobody paid much attention at first when static from the radio in the police car at the gate began to crackle; the sound hardly disturbed the buzz of the lazy afternoon. The police car was too far away to make out the words coming through. But then, when the car's motor was started, several people looked up. They could see Suzuki, who was walking near the gate with his laundry, being beckoned by the two policemen in the car.

After a brief discussion, Suzuki went to the gate, opened it wide so the car could get through, then left the gate open after the police car went through.

"It's over," Suzuki said as soon as he got close enough to be heard. "That radio message — the police said they caught their man. Leave the gate open, they said. Police chief told them to tell us we now could come and go as we please."

Who was arrested? The police did not say but no one was missing from the workers compound. The details of the case, spread by word of mouth, came later.

"Shit, you know what happened?" Fuzzy, who heard first, said. "The guy they arrested was some bum who worked the night shift in the cannery. Doesn't even look Oriental, I'm told."

"But how...?"

"You haven't heard the worst. It happened in some whorehouse on the edge of town. A sleazy dump, Nakano says. Guy didn't want to pay for 'extra service' or something. The Madame then apparently called the police. Guy got scared and took off. Didn't pay."

"But why'd they say one of us?"

"The Madame told the police the man was dark-skinned, had on work clothes; just assumed he was from the 'Jap camp.'"

Rape in a whorehouse? Jo wondered what they would come up with next.

But with the police case solved, talk about a strike ceased. By early evening a new work schedule for the week was posted on the mess hall bulletin board along with a notice that the Monday meeting of workers still would take place. The notice said the head of the WRA regional office in Denver would be present to hear any worker complaints and that work would resume with the afternoon shift.

The mess hall was full for the meeting. Jim, the foreman, stood on a makeshift platform up front, his hat off, showing blonde but very thin hair — maybe the reason why Jo never saw him before with his hat off. A middle-aged man, graying but thick-haired, sat next to him. Neither the police nor the deputy mayor were there.

"I know how some of you must feel," the middle-aged man said after he was introduced by the foreman as the director of the War Relocation Authority office in Denver. Jo didn't catch his name. The man's tone was conciliatory. "I represent your U.S. government, and therefore you. I've been told the details of the incident over the weekend and am here to listen to your grievances. Before we get started, however, I want to read a message I received just before I left Denver to come here. It's from my boss in Washington, Dillon S. Myer, the overall head of the War Relocation Authority. I'm sure you know that the WRA was established by the President specifically to look after the interests of the Japanese Americans. Mr. Myer, in case you did not know, has the ear of key people in the White House."

What crap, Jo thought, but listened as the man read: "Patriotic effort... great contribution to the world battle for democracy... grateful nation... true citizens."

When the man finished reading the message, he paused. Maybe he expected some cheers. Jim, the foreman, got up quickly and began clapping his hands and beckoning for others to join the applause.

Two or three of the workers followed suit, then there was silence.

"The message I just read is to you from Dillon S. Myer, who has direct contact with members of the President's cabinet in Washington," the WRA representative reiterated. "I hope all of you can appreciate its significance. It comes from the highest level and represents the true feelings of our — your — government. In addition to delivering Mr. Myer's message, I am here to listen to any of your grievances."

Grievances? Most of the workers still remained silent. Jo's feeling was that they were there to work and with the alleged rape case solved, they were going back to work. What else was there to gripe about?

One worker, who identified himself as a student from the University of Washington in Seattle, got up to complain about the "funny look" he got from the townspeople.

What a knucklehead, Jo thought. He might just as well complain about the whole war or the man in the moon; it was not something the WRA could do anything about.

Even as the student talked, the rest of the workers all seemed anxious to get back to their chores and the meeting, which now seemed quite irrelevant, broke up.

Sunday, a week later, the woman's charges of rape, the police cars in the compound, talk of a strike, the meeting in the mess hall — all seemed like history, something past and half forgotten. Jo, Fuzzy and two others from their crew, had gone to the drug store on the main street in town. They were leisurely making their way back to the compound when Jo noticed a group of townspeople up ahead by the bus stop. A dozen or so people stood on the sidewalk near the front door of a Greyhound bus that had just pulled in. The people were fidgeting; there were no smiles. Two women were openly in tears; worry showed on the faces of the men and other women.

Then Jo saw what it was about. A tall man in the olive drab uniform of the U.S. Army Air Corps, captain's bars on his shoulders and pilot's wing and Pacific Theater campaign ribbons on his chest, stepped down slowly from the bus. The top of the man's head was completely swathed in bandages, part of which also covered his left eye. To see out of his right eye, the man had to keep his face tilted upward, revealing young, pale-skinned features.

As the wounded man swung his head slowly to see who was there to greet him, he glanced over the heads of those around him, and suddenly was looking directly at Jo, now only about 10 yards away. Their eyes met. Then, with no show of emotion, the man turned his attention back to those immediately around him. A gray-haired woman, maybe his mother, began to embrace him.

In the brief second when Jo's and the airman's eyes met, several of the welcoming group turned their heads toward Jo and his companions. No words were spoken; though the looks conveyed resentment and hate.

Jo sympathized with the wounded man and his family. Rather than turn his head, however, Jo returned the sullen stares.

Back in the compound, Jo was restless. The <u>Newsweek</u> he had bought lay unopened on his bunk. He didn't even bother to take out the stationery for the letters he had been thinking of writing. Finally, Jo wandered to the far side of the bunkhouse where Takeda had a dice game going full swing, then climbed on a top bunk to watch.

Though he was on a bunk almost on top of the blanket-covered dice table, the roll of the dice, the occasional shout of *"shi-go-ro"* with a winning roll and the accompanying laughter seemed to come from far away.

Chapter Five
Flo

January 29, 1943: A War Department press release announces the registration program for both recruitment for military service and leave clearance. Niiya, Japanese American History, page 60.

February 6, 1943: Army teams were scheduled to visit the 10-WRA administered camps ... to register all male nisei of draft age. Each had to complete a special questionnaire, designed to test their "loyalty" and willingness to serve in the armed forces. ibid page 218.

O

Had things gone as they normally would have (if anything about camp living could be called normal) Flo probably would have had a good life. One happy aspect of the 10 relocation centers where the Japanese Americans were incarcerated during World War II was that hundreds of young men and women who ordinarily would not have even met each other did meet, fall in love and got married.

That was what seemed to be happening with Flo, a girl Jo knew from the time they were in the 6th grade at the Jefferson Union Elementary School in the rural area between Santa Clara and Sunnyvale south of San Francisco. Jo himself never looked at Flo in any romantic way. She was quiet and shy; did not do particularly well in school, maybe because of her shyness or because her English was not that good; had a fresh face that needed no cosmetics; always had a warm smile.

Jo and Flo went to the same high school and though they'd pass each other in the halls or see each other with separate groups after school while waiting for the bus, they rarely spoke beyond simple greetings.

When their families were interned at Santa Anita after the outbreak of World War II, Jo often would see Flo, or Flo's mother or father, or one of her two older brothers, or her younger sister. Flo's family was housed in the same row of horse stables as Jo's family and ate in the same "blue" mess hall — the mess halls at Santa Anita were identified by color and you were given mess tags of either red, blue, yellow, green, or orange according to the area of the camp you were housed in.

When they were moved to the Heart Mountain relocation center in Wyoming, their two families were in Block 9, only a few barracks removed from each other. Flo then worked as a waitress in the Block 9 mess hall.

Over all the years they had known each other, Jo never thought of Flo as being either pretty or not pretty; she was just the same friendly Flo. But two months or so after the families had been interned at Heart Mountain, they passed each other as Flo was going to work, and Jo, for the first time, noticed her in a different way. Her face was beaming (outside of a little lipstick, she still used no makeup). There seemed extra energy in her walk. She was tall for a Nisei girl — about five foot six or seven inches — and Jo could not help but notice her trim figure and the fair complexion behind the warm smile. It suddenly occurred to Jo that she was fairly attractive.

Maybe that's what love does, he thought. She had a boy friend, Hideo, a *kibei*, i.e. a *nisei* educated in Japan and then returned to America. Hideo, like a lot of the *kibe*, readjusting to life in America, was quiet and unobtrusive. Maybe his reserved manners were what attracted Flo to him.

Flo never introduced Hideo to Jo, but when she was with Hideo and they passed by Jo, she still smiled and said "hello" while Hideo would bow and smile. Sometimes Jo noticed them holding hands, but letting go as people approached. Outside of knowing his first name, Jo did not know much else about the man. He seemed a decent sort, and in time, whenever Jo passed Hideo, even if Flo was not with him, the man still would bow and smile.

Hideo drove the commissary truck that delivered food supplies to the mess halls on the eastern side of the camp where Block 9 was located. The rest of the truck crew probably was *Kibei* as well since they spoke to each other in Japanese, or, when they talked to the *Issei*, spoke a more proper form of the language than most *Nisei* were capable of.

Jo often saw Flo and Hideo sitting together on one of the mess hall's wooden dining tables having tea as Hideo's crew took a break from their commissary run. Hideo would be smoking his pipe, his olive drab cap and winter jacket on the bench by his side. He had a stocky build, wore circular steel-rimmed glasses emphasizing his round eyes and round face, a face that women probably saw as very cute when the man was a baby. He and Flo made a good-looking couple and had they not been in camp, they probably would not have waited very long to get married. Or maybe they were even making arrangements to get married while in camp.

Jo didn't know when the romance between the two started. He had been going in and out of camp on temporary releases, first to top sugar beets in Montana and then to harvest beans in nearby Powell, Wyoming. But by Christmas of 1942, the romance was going strong.

The winter of 1942-43 at Heart Mountain was severe, or maybe all winters there were that severe. At 20 degrees or so below zero moisture would freeze on the hair in Jo's nostrils when he breathed in. That Christmas brought the first deep snow — about a foot — that Jo was to experience.

If anything, though, the winter harshness seemed to have made the romance between Flo and her boy friend that much cozier. Jo noticed, for instance, that while walking outside in the cold wind, the two now kept their arms around each other for warmth and support even when people passed, no longer bothering to hide their feelings for each other as they had done earlier.

The snow that Christmas gave more meaning to Bing Crosby's singing of "A White Christmas," the song that was played almost without stop on radios in the barracks or the camp's loudspeaker systems. Jo felt that people at Heart Mountain were getting more used to camp life, emotions seemed more settled.

Shortly after the holiday season, however, news from Washington about separating "loyal" from "disloyal" internees shattered whatever harmony was being established. Each person in camp over 17 years old would have to fill out a questionnaire drawn up for that purpose, the reports said. The Army recruitment drive and the assumption that eligible *Nisei* would soon be subject again to the Army draft added to the turmoil.

Jo went to the meetings held in the administrative barracks where the reasons for the questionnaires and the new Army recruitment policy were explained by a team of two officers and three enlisted men. These meetings were followed up by meetings among the internees alone in various mess halls throughout the camp.

In Jo's area, joint meetings between neighboring Blocks 8 and 9 were held in the Block 8 mess hall. When Jo arrived at the mess hall at 7:30 p.m., the scheduled time for the initial block meeting, the mess hall already was packed. Wives and girl friends had come with the men. All of the seats of the two dozen dining room tables were taken and people stood elbow to elbow along the sides and back aisle in the smoke-filled room. Some even sat on the stainless steel serving counters.

"We of Block 8 have decided to stick together, refuse to fill in the loyalty questionnaire or cooperate with the Army in its recruitment drive until our rights are restored," the first of many speakers announced. Jo didn't know the man, sensed his anger, but wondered what right the man had to speak for others in the block on something Jo thought each person had to decide for himself.

Others followed, most also venting their frustrations and asking questions for which there were no immediate answers. When could a man expect a draft notice if he answered "yes" to the loyalty questions? Would families whose sons volunteered or were drafted then be allowed to return home? What if a person refuses to answer the questions?

The initial block meeting went on until midnight, and eventually, after about two dozens speakers, a resolution to ask the administrators for some statement on the restoration of basic rights was moved but not passed and left for further action the next evening. No consensus could be reached on the wording of the resolution.

Though Jo stayed until the meeting ended, he felt that any resolution issued by people of Blocks 8 and 9 would mean little; who in Washington was going to pay any attention to it? Besides, the important decisions probably were already made.

But as he stood in the crowded rooms, Jo felt left out. Since he was born in Japan, technically he was an *Issei*, and, whether he liked it or not, a Japanese national, not a "non-alien Japanese" as the *Nisei* had been identified by the officials. He wasn't going to volunteer for anything, though deep down he wished that he would have had to face the draft like the *Nisei* his age.

He was given the questionnaire issued by the civilian War Relocation Authority to the *Issei* parents and *Nisei* woman, not the questionnaire given to the male *Nisei*. The questionnaire for the male *Nisei* asked the same questions, but was issued by the War Department and carried the seal of Selective Service System. Sure, he would serve in the U.S. armed forces like the *Nisei* if required, Jo felt. He'd go if they drafted him. But he knew his draft status would remain that of an enemy alien — 4-C. The questionnaire asked him to "forswear any allegiance or obedience to the Japanese emperor" when he never felt any allegiance to the emperor to begin with. As Jo listened to the speakers at the block meeting, he already had made up his mind to answer neither of the two "loyalty" questions and let whatever was to happen, just happen.

It was not until the initial block meeting was ending that Jo noticed Flo and Hideo at one of the front tables, talking to Flo's two brothers and people Jo didn't recognize. Jo could not hear what they were saying, but he could see the shaking of heads and animated hand gestures.

More block meetings, again often late into the night, followed. Though Jo had made up his own mind, the turmoil among his friends continued as they agonized over what choices to make. Tom Suzuki, the only son of a gardener, for example, spent days talking to Jo and others. His parents were getting older; thought that if they answered "no" to the loyalty questions they could remain in camp and eventually be repatriated to Japan. Tom had never been to Japan, spoke only limited Japanese. Tom wanted to get out of camp, get his degree in microbiology, go on to medical school. But in the end Tom decided he couldn't leave his parents and acquiesced to his parents' wishes.

Jimmy Watanabe, another high school friend, signed up within days of the recruiting teams arrival, contrary to his parents wishes. Jimmy was taken outside of camp with the first group to take the Army physical, only to be rejected.

Not too long after the Army recruitment team had left camp and before the stir caused by the loyalty questionnaire had died down, a new phenomenon occurred. Throughout the camp, women, each with a piece of cloth and needle and thread in hand, went from mess hall to mess hall stopping other women as they came out.

At first Jo did not know what it was about, then learned that the women were following an old Japanese custom: they were preparing *sennin-bari* — sashes with a thousand stitches, each stitch sewn by a different woman. Such sashes were to be worn by soldiers going off to war. Myth had it that the sash would protect the soldier from enemy bullets. In the modern sense it simply meant that the wishes of a thousand women went with the soldier for his safe return.

Though the women waiting outside the mess hall doors were discreet about it — there were only two or three women at the door at any one time — it was easy to see whose sons or sweethearts had volunteered.

Jo was not surprised when he saw Flo and her mother standing outside the mess hall door at Block 9. Her oldest brother, Frank, had made it clear that he wanted to prove his loyalty to America by answering the Army's call for volunteers. Jo assumed that the sash was for Frank. (The second brother, Kaz, was just as adamant in declaring he would resist the draft when it was reinstated for the *Nisei.*)

But when he got close enough, Jo could see that Flo's face was tear-stained. Why? Jo wondered. Rather than look his way, Flo turned, perhaps to hide her misery. He didn't stop to ask anything and upset her further.

Some calmness seemed to return to the camp at Heart Mountain as the weeks became months of waiting for the next official move. In late April Jo signed up to cut asparagus and then harvest peas for the Blue Mountain Canneries in the eastern part of Washington State. After returning to camp in mid-summer, he went out again on temporary release as a laborer with a construction crew laying the foundation for Elk Basin, a village in the oil fields of northern Wyoming; then went to Worland, a small farming community in the north central part of the state, to help repair an irrigation canal.

Though the crew returned to the camp on weekends from Elk Basin and Worland, Jo lost track of what was happening in camp. On these weekends, he noticed that Flo no longer worked in the Block 9 mess hall and asked Ayako, whose family also was from Santa Clara.

"Didn't you know?" Ayako said. "She and Hideo went to Tule Lake."

"Oh?" Jo said. The camp at Tule Lake was the camp where the so-called "disloyals" now were being held.

"Being 'loyal' or 'disloyal' had nothing to do with it," Ayako said. She said Flo and Hideo got married and seemed to be doing all right as far as Ayako knew from a letter she had received from Flo. Flo said she was looking forward to going to Japan, where Hideo had relatives, but who knows when.

"That's not the sad part," Ayako said. "Flo originally was reluctant to go because her family was being split three ways."

Flo's brother Frank now was taking Army basic training in Camp Shelby, Mississippi, Ayako said, while the second brother Kaz was actively involved with a group organized to protest the registration of *Nisei* for the Selective Service.

"Kaz has vowed to and will probably go to prison for resisting the draft," Ayako said. "Their poor mother is beside herself...says she feels she no longer has a family; that she no longer knows where she and her husband can go or what they will be able to do once the camp is closed."

Jo never learned what eventually happened to Flo or the rest of her family. He sometimes wondered if Flo and Hideo ever made it back to Japan, and if they did, how they fared in post-war Japan.

Flo, Jo always felt, should have had a good life; he hoped she did.

Chapter Six
Wyoming

Aug. 12, 1942: The first "Volunteers" arrive at Heart Mountain, Wyo. In September the demand for seasonal workers from the centers increased enormously; by mid-October 10,000 evacuees were on seasonal leave ... when the harvest ended, the Nisei were credited with having saved the sugar beet crops of several Western states. (Niiya, Japanese American History, page 348-9)

June, 1943: "Now that the nisei in the camps and on the battlefield were in no position to protect their interests, the state of California began the seizure of evacuee-held land...Forthwith declared illegal were properties purchased by the Issei in the name of their citizen children..." (Michi Weglyn, Years of Infamy, Wm. Morrow & Co. Inc. New York, 1976, page 152.

○

KISA

Sell the farm? Kisa was taken aback.

Until then, his shared ownership of the farm, he felt, protected him and his family from the uncertainties of where they would be and what they would be doing once out of camp. He had assumed that once the war was over the two families, they and the Kiyonos, would be able to return to the farm in California and resume where they had left off.

Now, suddenly, he was being told that they would have no farm or home to return to.

"*Shikata-ganai* — we don't have much choice," Ken said. Ken Kiyono was the eldest son of the family sharing the farm with Kisa's family. The farm, being bought under a ten-year mortgage, was under Ken's name since Kisa and his Japan-born children could not own land in California.

Kisa had returned a few days earlier to the Heart Mountain relocation center from topping sugar beets on a farm near Riverton, a small town in central Wyoming. Now that he was back, he had gone to visit Ken's parents, and then dropped in to see Ken, who with his wife and three-year-old son, were housed in the same barracks.

Ken did not waste any time giving Kisa the bad news, though Kisa could be see by the younger man's expression that Ken was as troubled by what he was going to say as he knew Kisa would be.

Ken said he had just gotten a letter from Frank Belli, who was supposed to farm the land and make the mortgage payments in lieu of rent while the two families were away.

Belli, Ken said, wrote that he (Belli) had been told that the state was to begin a check on all farms in California whose owners had Japanese names. Any property which was listed under false ownership or involved in any attempt to skirt the state's ban on land ownership by aliens would be confiscated.

With the anti-Japanese sentiment on the West Coast stronger than ever, Belli said, who knows what may come about? Belli said he did not want to risk becoming involved in any possible prosecution by the state. Therefore, Belli said, he would continue to run the farm only if the property is sold to him.

"We have to trust the man," Ken said, though he had no way of knowing whether what Belli said was true. But Belli knew that Kisa and his family were using Ken's name to get around the California land laws, Ken said. If Belli were called to testify he would have to tell the truth.

"If the state decides that our arrangements are illegal, they could take away our property and leave us with nothing," Ken said. "Even if the state does not act, without Belli we have no way of keeping up the mortgage payments. If we sell, like Belli insists, we at least will get back some of the money we've put in."

Maybe Belli should not have been trusted in the first place, Kisa thought. However, Belli, who trucked the produce from the farm to the wholesale market in San Francisco, knew Ken from grammar school days. There had been very little time to prepare for the evacuation; there was no choice but to trust whoever was available.

"I know how much it must hurt," Ken said. "My parents are also upset. I'm sorry."

Kisa nodded, but saw no need for Ken to apologize. After all, Kisa said, he and his family would not have been able to be on the farm to begin with but for the use of Ken's name. Being in camp, there was little more they could do.

As Kisa made his way back across the camp to his own barracks, he thought over what Ken had said. It was still snowing, and cold. The tiny flakes came down sideways, swirling like dust in the wind before settling in small banks behind poles or by the sides of the barracks. Kisa, who earlier had marvelled at the dryness of the snow — it reminded him of the

19th century water color paintings of Hiroshige — now hardly notice the powdery flakes.

Selling the farm meant that what he and his family had worked for since their arrival in America 18 years before was going to naught. He felt now that he had been naive in his optimism and trust.

During the two-month period just prior to the evacuation, for example, the two families prepared the farm for Belli's takeover. Belli wanted to grow sugar beets instead of more labor intense crops such as celery, string beans, pole peas and other produce. The plots on the 40 acres were plowed and rearranged into larger ones more suitable for the beets and the beets were planted. The underground irrigation pipes were mended; the road leading into the farm re-gravelled. The Ford-Ferguson tractor on which Kisa had just finished paying the last installment was left for Belli to use.

Neither family received any money for the work done or for the tractor or other equipment left behind, since Belli supposedly was doing the two families a favor.

What hurt Kisa was not the lost time or the lost effort; it was being completely helpless and unable to even lift a finger while what he and his family had worked so hard for was being taken away. Ah well, Kisa thought, and caught himself before he let the bitterness take too strong a hold.

He didn't blame Ken; he didn't even want to blame Belli. He could even excuse being in camp. The country was at war; he was an enemy alien. Any action taken by U.S. authorities could be justified. Any losses he suffered would have to be lived with.

Up to now, Kisa had looked on the evacuation and internment, first, in the horse stables at Santa Anita and then, Heart Mountain , as way stations on his family's temporary removal from their California home. His assumption that they would be able to return home had made it easy to take most things in stride. In the beet field, for instance, it was bend and chop, bend and chop, through rows of beets several hundred yards long. His back ached. It was piece work — a dollar for each ton topped — and since the beets were small, each of the crew earned less then $100 for the entire the five weeks they were there. They slept in an old railway boxcar on the edge of the field. For Kisa, though, the hardship was well worth being out of the camp. He was free to come and go as he pleased. He could go into Riverton, buy some beer, get a steak, eat what he pleased. The money earned made little difference as far as his overall situation was concerned; some day he would be back on his own farm.

The possibility that the family might not be able to return to the farm was always there — who could foresee what would happen because of the war — but Kisa had not given that serious thought. At times he had even felt smug as he listened to his camp neighbors who had no homes to return to once the camps were closed. Now he, like they, was without a home.

Kisa tried to rationalize. Pretend life was a poker game; he and his wife had gambled on the farm and had lost.

Try as he would, however, he could not just shrug off the years of toil — his, his wife's, the children's — and doing without. Just a half dozen more years and the farm could have been paid for. Pretending did not really ease the pain. As he walked, Kisa turned his thoughts away from what might have been — why continue to aggravate himself. He turned his thoughts to poems he had been composing in his head.

He and his wife had joined a poetry group when they first arrived in Heart Mountain. In the beet fields in Riverton, the soil under his feet, the smell of freshly-turned earth, distant calls of a pheasant and the cooing of doves, the nip in the air signaling the approach of colder weather — all reminded Kisa of his own farm. The reminders were bitter-sweet, contained seeds of ideas he could play with and put into a *tanka*, then take to the group's readings.

He remembered seeing the plow which dug up the beets hit an ant nest, causing the tiny creatures to scurry about trying to bring order out of chaos. For an ant the task at that moment probably was as formidable as it was for a human looking for order in the world at war. The germ of an idea.

Those returning to the camp from the beet fields had to go through an inspection for contraband before being allowed in. No matter how many times Kisa went through such an inspection, and though he never had anything to hide, he always was revolted by this invasion of his privacy. He wondered if he could put into the metered requirements of *tanka* the irony of having had to submit to this humiliation while returning to camp and giving up his freedom.

The wind and the cold numbed his cheeks as he walked. A skilled poet, he thought, might use the winter harshness as a metaphor to express his sense of loss. He played with other ideas.

When he returned to the barracks of Block 9, though, he knew he would have to tell his wife that they were losing their home. For the time being, there was little else he could tell her. He didn't know when or where they might go when they left the camp permanently.

He'd continue writing his poetry, but the future now hung like the sword over his head.

○

JANICE

For her, it was like a story book romance. Lt. Tom T. Okada. He looked so handsome in his crisp olive-drab uniform. He was much more handsome than Gregory Peck, for instance, who had starred in the movie she had seen at the recreation barracks the other night. What was the title — "Twelve O'Clock High?" Anyway her Tom had a pointed nose like Gregory Peck, the same black hair, of course, and was thin and tall for a Japanese. But Tom was much younger. She wrung her hands and, unconsciously, was looking up at the ceiling when a voice interrupted her daydreaming.

"Janice — thinking of your future, are you?" the kindly voice said.

"Oh...," Janice responded, her face turning red for she was caught completely by surprise. "Mrs. Sato. I...er ...I was..."

"Never you mind. All I need is to have this prescription filled. Then you can go back to dreaming of your Tom. I've heard only good things about him."

"Oh, Mrs. Sato, I didn't see you come in. I..."

"Now, now. No need to apologize," the older woman said. "I've been talking to your mother. Two weeks. 'It's such a short time,' your mother says. She says you seem to be so much in love. 'But two weeks. Can they really know each other?'"

"I know," Janice said. "Two weeks is such a short time. But he's only got two more weeks of leave left. He says he can't, we can't, wait. He..."

"Janice. Janice dear. I'm not your mother. You don't have to explain or justify anything to me. I'm a family friend; your mother's, yours. Maybe it's true love. Maybe just infatuation. Who knows? I've been married to that husband of mine for 30 years. But love? Infatuation? I'm not sure I know the difference even now."

"But it has to be more. I'm sure of myself. Tom is too. We've spent almost all of our time together talking about the future. It's got to be."

"I'm sure it will be," Mrs. Sato said as she reached for the little white bag with the prescription the pharmacist handed to Janice through the window. "You're so young. I pray to God that you have time to find out."

Without saying anything further, Mrs. Sato leaned over the counter and kissed Janice's cheek, then left. Janice could not help but notice the tears in the older woman's eyes.

She, Janice Shirai; she'd be Janice Okada soon. They planned a very simple wedding. It'd be in the chapel which had been converted from one of the barracks. Her sister would be the lone bridesmaid. Tom's Army buddy, who was coming in from Camp Shelby, would be the best man. There'd be just the two families; Dr. Nakano, who got her the job at the camp hospital, and her best friend from grade school days, Amy, Mrs. Sato's daughter. She felt bad. She would have liked to invite more. But being in camp, there was no way. Her friends understood.

As she thought of the wedding, she felt the pressure of time. For more than two years, she had more time than she knew what to do with. In camp everyone seem to have time on their hands, even those who had camp jobs, found hobbies, painted, wrote *haiku*, read, or just wandered around. No matter what it was they did, everyone also was waiting — to relocate, to return to their homes, to get permanent exit permits, to be accepted by a school — waiting to get on with their lives.

For her, Tom's arrival was like a gale sweeping in from the outside. Now everything was rush, rush, rush.

Tom had come to Heart Mountain to see his family before he went overseas. The Okada's were from the Los Angeles area, her family from the Bay area. She and Tom only met by chance. He had taken his mother to the hospital pharmacy. Janice was reluctant when, out of the blue, he asked for a date. Normally, she would have just turned up her nose. But he seemed to be so lonely, lost among those in camp, seeking something, so she agreed to see him after work. Marriage was the last thing on her mind then. But...

Her mother was rushing around frantically — she needed material for the wedding dresses, had to make last minute arrangements for Rev. Suzuki to officiate, got a camp chef to promise a special wedding dinner for the families. Her mother was not going to let her daughter spend her wedding night in camp and was getting a temporary leave permit so her daughter could spend a short honeymoon in nearby Cody.

Janice could not explain how things happened so quickly. But now she wanted to spend every hour, no, even every minute with Tom before he had to leave. Time, suddenly, had become so precious.

O

MIYO

"Heart Mountain? Wyoming?" the woman at the railway depot in Denver asked. After several minutes of checking through the train schedules in front of her, she shook her head. "Can't find it. Never heard of it. Some kind of camp? Let me ask my boss."

Then a man, fat, wearing the trousers and cap of a railway official, but a plaid shirt, not part of his uniform, came out.

"Some kind of Jap camp?" the man asked, then before Miyo could say anything, went on, "Leona's checked all of the station listings in Wyoming. I remember reading something in the newspapers ... but we don't have any such station listed. Sorry, can't help."

Miyo was upset, annoyed that the railroad official made no further effort as he returned to his desk in the back room.

"Gosh, now what do we do?" she asked as she turned toward her husband. Poor Ed, she thought, here he was trying to get used to being in uniform and worried about reporting to his training camp in time. He didn't need the added aggravations of this trip.

The decision to visit her family in camp was made at the last minute. Ed had just finished dental school at Washington University in St. Louis and then was inducted into the Army. He had five days before he was to report to the Army training center at Camp Shelby in Mississippi. It would have been an easy trip from St. Louis to Camp Shelby, but he agreed to make the trip to Wyoming if, for no other reason, than to give her some peace of mind. They were working out the details of their travel as they went. After a day and a night on a train, they were in Denver, but now no one could tell them how to get to where they were going.

"What kine nonsense dis?" Ed asked, reverting to the Pidgin English of his native Hawaii as the railroad official left. Ed used Pidgin purposely when annoyed. "Bugger the *haole* bastard. Hell, they can't just lock up 10,000 people somewhere in Wyoming then not know how to get there. Let's ask around, try the phone book, call any Japanese name listed. Someone's got to know."

As they made their way toward the phone booths through the scattering of men in uniform and women and children either greeting or seeing them off, Miyo saw an Asian girl entering the depot from a train arrival gate. As they got closer, to Miyo's surprise and delight, she recognized the face, that of an old high school classmate, someone she hadn't seen for a half dozen years. As it was, the classmate had just returned to Denver from Heart Mountain after seeing her family there. She not only knew how to get to the camp, but had the train schedule to Billings, Montana, and the bus schedule from there to Cody and Powell in Wyoming, the two towns closest to the camp at Heart Mountain.

It's a prison camp. The thought intruded into the Miyo's swirl of emotions as she stepped off of the bus at the gate to Heart Mountain. The bus had stopped five or six yards outside of the gate and its sentry post. She had to squeeze between the seats toward the bus door. Then, when she stepped outside and looked up, the stark reality of what she saw struck her.

About two dozen people from the camp were standing inside the gate to greet the half dozen visitors who had just arrived. What she saw seemed exactly like newsreel scenes of prisoner-of-war camps in Europe and Asia — the gate and the barbed wire; people wearing a mixture of surplus military and civilian clothes (fatigues, scruffy navy hats, and "Ike" jackets with jeans, faded windbreakers and flannel shirts); the M.P. with his white helmet and black armband.

Behind the gate, she could see the camp above a bluff at the next higher level of gray-brown foothills with smoke from the soft coal burned in hundreds of pot-bellied stoves adding a haze. The barbed wire stretched off into the foothills on both sides of the gate.

It took her several moments before she adjusted to the scene; then, when she looked back at those by the gate she recognized her younger brother and two younger sisters. She waved as she approached them, then fought back tears. The group seemed so destitute.

Until then Miyo was full of questions about the camps. The letters to her, first from Santa Anita, then Heart Mountain, were from the younger brother — her parents didn't write since she couldn't read Japanese — and gave almost no details. What she knew came mostly from letters received by others who also had relatives in the camps and occasional items in the newspapers which seemed to report only camp unrests such as that in Santa Anita, Manzanar and Poston.

During her trip from St. Louis she had been excited — elated — with the anticipation of seeing her family. She had been saving up so much to tell them, especially her mother — about the wedding, her and Ed's future plans, about life in St. Louis, people she had met. There was so much she wanted to know about how they were faring, what the plans were for the future.

But the camp, the barbed wire ...

Miyo's stay in Heart Mountain was just overnight. The visit, like a dream, seemed over before it even got started. The next evening Miyo and her husband were on a bus headed back to Billings. In the darkness, Miyo caught a glimpse of the camp through the window as the bus moved up and around the curves on the road through the mountains. No other lights were visible, and from afar, the camp lights, in straight lines marking off each block, stood out in the night like jewels. If she had not known what she was looking at, she might have marveled at the sight: a new town maybe? A fairground? Some carefully laid out defense plant? But she knew, and the very orderliness of the lights seemed a mockery of her unsettled emotions.

The family's barracks room 9-5-E (Block 9, Building 5, Room E), sheets hung on clothes lines to divide the spaces for each of the army cots where they slept, the laundry building with women in line waiting their turns to use the toilets and showers, the pile of coal dumped on each of end of the rows of barracks, the crying of babies amid the clang of metal trays and the rancid smell in the mess hall — all were like blurred photographs, which, just momentarily, had been real.

She was glad, of course, that she had the chance to see her family. They seemed healthy enough. But how long could they stay in the camp? Where could they go? Her father and mother hardly spoke English. Without the farm what would they be able to do?

None of the worry Miyo felt showed in her family. Her mother and father, the brother who was practice teaching in the camp's junior high school, and her two younger sisters seemed to be taking the whole experience in stride. (The two other brothers had already left camp, one for Chicago, the other New York.) Camp life appeared to lull those left behind into a false sense of security. There'd be nobody to feed or house them when they had to return to the outside; maybe nobody would even give them a job.

She wanted to discuss her feelings with Ed, her husband. But she feared losing control of her emotions, of ending up just crying.

Miyo half dozed off as the bus moved on. In her moments of sleep, she dreamt. In the dream she heard a radio newscaster speak of Heart Mountain, saying that the "relocation center" was, for the time being, Wyoming's third largest city. The voice sounded like that of her brother, who, when she and her husband had arrived at the camp, gave them all of the camp's statistics. Then the fat clerk supervisor at the train depot in Denver came on, "Some kind of Jap camp? Jap Camp? Jap Camp?" His voice seemed to echo, and then she relived her first reaction on seeing the camp just the day before. She struggled but was unable to rid herself of the notion that Heart Mountain was a prison camp, and, like the railway official, most of America did not know or care.

○

KISA

"Chick Sexers — Good Wages after Training," the poster on the wall in the camp's employment office read. Good money, maybe, Kisa thought, but shook his head. He could picture what the work must be like — rows of booths, strong lights, people in white coats hunched over peeping bundles of fluffy feathers. It couldn't be healthy.

He thumbed through the list of job offerings for the *Issei*, but saw nothing new. The choices for the older generation with limited use of English were few. It was a list much shorter than that for the younger *Nisei*.

What did he want? He wasn't sure what sort of job he could get. He was sure though, that with no home to return to, he wanted to get out of camp as soon as possible and get started on whatever future was in store.

He would have preferred somewhere close of New York where his older children had gone. He could farm, and a large agro-business in New Jersey which sold frozen foods nationwide was recruiting. Many families had already signed up to go there. Kisa felt, however, that it would be like moving from camp to what would be another "Japanese colony."

Sharecroppers were needed in the South. The employment counselor assured everyone that in the South their children would go to schools for the white children, not those for the Negroes. But Kisa wondered, would he be comfortable being treated as white in a segregated community?

Though Kisa visited the employment office regularly, the opportunity to leave camp came, not from the employment office but from a former student of his years ago at the emigrants school in Tokyo. The student, who also had worked on Kisa's farm in California while attending graduate school, had since earned his degree in chemistry and was working for a drug company in Holland, Michigan. The co-owner of the drug company lived on a farm a few miles out of town on the shores of Lake Michigan and was looking for a couple: a man to tend the land and a woman to cook and help with housework.

On the surface, the offer seemed ideal — housing, on the lake shore, a small but good school nearby, and no need to worry about rationing since the owner, classified as a farmer, got whatever gas and sugar he needed, and butchered his own meat.

It was late April, 1944, when the final arrangements to leave camp were made.

On the day they were leaving, Kisa gave one last look at the empty room in the barracks. The mattresses were rolled up on the iron cots and the curtains taken down. The room again suddenly felt bare. He looked at the two small stools and the bench he had fashioned out of wood he had salvaged from the scrap lumber pile at the edge of camp. Without the cushions Yoshi had made for them, they looked naked. But he had spent hours making the simple furniture using just a hand saw, plane, and hammer and nails. He had gotten used to the furniture and felt a loss because they would have to be left behind.

Outside, Kisa could hear his wife talking to the neighbors. Though many of the neighbors' older sons and daughters had already left camp, she and Kisa were among the first of the older generation to strike out on their own.

"Heh?" and "Hmm" were the reactions when the neighbors were told that he and Yoshi with their youngest daughter were moving to Michigan, miles away from their children in New York. He and Yoshi would have liked to be closer to the children. But they were determined, first, to live their own lives, and second, not to be a burden to their children.

As they were saying their final goodbyes before boarding the truck which was to take them to the bus stop at the gate, Kisa remembered another departure more than 40 years before when he left his native village in the southern Japan Alps for Tokyo. He felt the same excitement now as he did then, of moving on to a new life. However, he was now in his mid-fifties, not a 14-year-old.

The Author with Coach John J. Walsh (right) and team-mates of the University of Wisconsin boxing team in Miami in March, 1947, prior to bouts with the University of Miami boxing team.

Posted photo of the author in the University of Wisconsin boxing team uniform (Spring, 1946).

Chapter Seven
The Referee

Aug. 31, 1944: The War Department lifts all restrictions on colleges Nisei are allowed to enroll in. (Japanese American History, page 64.)

O

Jo at back on his stool, leaning against the corner ropes as Max, the team manager and trainer, pulled and shook Jo's arms and massaged the muscles to keep them loose while the coach hovered over him.

"How you feeling?" Tom, the coach, asked as the ammonia from the smelling salt in his right hand went sharply up Jo's nose.

"Fine. But the ref..."

"Yeah, that damn ref," the coach nodded.

"Hell, you still have to be way ahead on points," Max asserted.

"Sure," the coach said. "But we've got to do more to win this one." Then as he turned his head toward the referee — balding, middle-aged — said, "Let me think."

In the background, Jo could hear the murmur of the wartime crowd. Five hundred? A thousand? He couldn't tell how many. They were mostly Navy people, but unlike the other World War II Navy bases at Bunker Hill, Indiana, and Ottumwa, Iowa, where the team had fought before, this was Penn State College so co-eds were scattered among the audience. Earlier, as he had walked down the dimly-lit aisle to the ring, he sensed more curiosity than hostility, but still kept his eyes focused straight ahead.

"Think I got it," the coach said, finally. "Sucker him in. Start like you usually do. Get in close. Not your style, but when he starts throwing, take a step back, make him come to you."

"I'll try," Jo said as the coach replaced Jo's rubber mouthpiece and moved out of the ring with the sound of the buzzer.

The third and final round. Jo was up immediately with the bell and moving toward his opponent. As they circled, Jo watched the man's face closely. He had pale skin and freckles, a pointed nose and a pointed chin, thin lips, light blue eyes. The man tried to keep his face deadpan, but an occasional fluttery blink indicated anxiety. From the corner of his eyes, Jo could see the referee off to the side.

As Jo moved in, he saw the left jab coming and caught it easily on his left shoulder. He countered with a jab, a quick right and another left. He saw the grimace on his opponent's face as the man's head was jerked back. Maybe I can finish it now, Jo thought as he shuffled forward. Then he heard the shout, "Break," as the arms of the referee — pin-striped sleeves rolled up to the elbows — came between him and his opponent.

When they squared off again, Jo could see his opponent was still on the defensive. When the man put out a feeler jab, Jo stopped. The man jabbed again, then followed with a right, neither of which landed, as Jo stepped back as the coach had suggested. Surprised, the man moved forward, throwing punches with both hands which Jo blocked easily with his gloves and elbows. The man couldn't hit hard, wasn't even scoring legitimate points, but the crowd suddenly burst into cheers.

Hell, Jo thought, they don't know what boxing is. He could have stood there all day and let the man throw punches that way without Jo really getting hit or even arm weary.

As the man kept coming, Jo set himself, and when the man finished his flurry, Jo moved in quickly. For the moment, he forgot the war, the crowd, the coach, the referee, everyone and everything around him but his opponent. Jo hit, blocked, hit, leaned in, swung, ducked, and hit again. He laughed to himself in exuberance as he felt the rhythm of his blows, the solid impact as they landed.

Then, suddenly, he felt his opponent weakening, starting to fall back, wobbly. Jo sensed the crowd again. There was a sudden hush, and Jo could hear his coach shout, "Go, lad, go."

Then, as suddenly, the hairy arms with the rolled-up sleeves were again between him and his opponent.

"Break," Jo heard.

"Christ," Jo said as he glanced at the referee.

"I said 'break,'" the referee responded without even looking up as his arms pushed the fighters apart.

Jo tried to repeat the tactic his coach had suggested, but his opponent was wary now, wouldn't move in. Jo got him in a corner once, but the referee was there again. In what seemed no time, the bell ended the round.

Max and the coach had already climbed into the ring and were waiting as Jo went to his corner.

"Your idea worked for a while," Jo said as the coach covered Jo's head with a towel and Max draped a robe over Jo's shoulders.

"Hell, you had him out on his feet; could've finished him but for the ref," the coach said.

Jo watched the coach's face as they waited for the referee's decision. Something was bothering the coach; something more than just what had happened in the ring. He could see it in the coach's frown; the way he looked at the referee.

The referee, the sole judge of the bout, soon was in the center of the ring beckoning the two fighters, then raising the sailor's right gloved hand, announced, "The winner — Seaman Robert J. Fields."

The crowd was silent — it took a second or two for the announcement to soak in — then burst into cheers.

"That bastard," Jo heard the coach saying when he reached the corner, then repeat, "that bastard." And for the first time since Jo had known him, Jo saw a glimpse of meanness in the coach's eyes as he looked at the referee.

"A real home-towner," Max volunteered. "Don't feel too bad, Jo, these things happen."

"Yeah, we know that," the coach said. "But..." He was about the say more, but stopped.

The next day the team was on a train headed for Chicago where they would change trains for Madison. Most of the eight-member team was lounging around in their seats — playing cards, talking or just watching the scenery. The coach and Max sat together at the front of the car.

Jo, the lone civilian on the team, was on a seat by himself, trying to catch up on some reading. He had missed two days of classes; he could at least try to keep up with the required reading. The others on the team were in the Navy, either at the radio and radar school at the University of Wisconsin, or in the Navy's V-12 Program. Only one of them, Kowalski, the light heavyweight, had brought along some books as well, but these remained unopened.

"Oh Hell, you can't study on this train," Kowalski said as he sat next to Jo. "We'll be home in another four or five hours; might as well wait until then."

"I suppose," Jo said as he put his book down. "Haven't been able to concentrate anyway. Got to get it done, though."

"Know how you feel," Kowalski said. "But don't take things so seriously. Relax. I used to be like you; kept worrying about homework, the tests, my grades. But Hell, you're young; you've got time."

"You're probably right," Jo smiled. He was being told by Kowalski that he, Jo, was young. Jo was 20 years old; Kowalski exactly 21. Kowalski — blond haired and blue eyed — looked a lot like the U.S. sailor pictured on recruiting posters.

"The hell with the books," Kowalski said suddenly, and the two of them started to laugh.

"Glad you have things to laugh about," a voice above them in the aisle said. It was the coach who had come back unnoticed from the front end of the car. "How you guys back here keeping."

"No problems," Kowalski said.

"Let me get back to you after I've had a word with the others," the coach said as he moved on.

Jo watched the coach, Thomas B. Kelly, move up the aisle. Kelly grew up in a rough part of Chicago, Jo was told. Heavily built, and since he was not longer in training, a bit fat. Despite his weight and height — he was about 6 foot, 2 or so inches — he still moved light on his feet and had a snap to his punches. Jo had watched him work out on the bags a couple of times after the team had finished its workout. Kelly had had 50 or more fights and was once ranked among the top ten heavyweights in the country, according to a newspaper account Jo read when the coach was first appointed.

The coach sat opposite Jo and Kowalski when he returned.

"Jo," he said, "when we get back to town I'm going to call the newspapers and tell them about the bum deal the ref gave you. I want to tell everyone that you should not have that loss on your record. I'll call Anderson at the Cap times and what's his name at the Journal as well. I'm sure they'll run what I tell them."

The coach's round, smooth-skinned face turned red as he talked. Even his small nose — twisted almost into an "S" shape when it was broken in his last fight — changed color.

"Like Max said, those things happen," Jo said.

"But this was something special," the coach said. "You know I've been in the ring often enough. Had some bad hometown decisions along the way, too. But what happened last night made me mad, and the more I thought about it, the madder I got. Couldn't sleep until I had made up my mind on what to do. Kowalski, you saw it. What did you think?"

"Stunk all right," Kowalski said.

"See. Ask anyone. You'll get the same answer," the coach said. "Got to get back to my seat now; start adding up the expenses with Max. But first I wanted to tell you about how bad I felt and what I've decided to do about it."

"Thanks," Jo said as the coach got up.

"That's it, keep your chin tucked in," the coach said as he playfully jabbed at Jo's face. "We'll get them the next time."

"Never seen him as upset about a decision," Kowalski said as the coach moved away. "He's not just putting on a show to make you feel better. You really had the guy beat bad."

"Yeah, it's really bugging him," Jo said.

"Hey," Kowalski said, changing the subject, "I'm going to the club car to get a coke. Why don't you come along?"

"Naw," Jo said, "got to finish this chapter."

"Can I get you something, then?"

"Yeah, coffee. Thanks."

After Kowalski got up, Jo opened his economics book to restart the chapter on marginal enterprises. But he still couldn't concentrate, and instead was soon looking out of the window at the passing countryside.

Must still be Ohio, he thought, as he looked out at the barren winter scene. Patches of snow were snuggled against fences on the edge of empty fields. Large red barns, tall silos, and large white houses amid groves of high trees showed that the area had to be good farming country. They reminded him of what used to be his home.

His thoughts went back to the coach. A good man. Two months back Jo lost his job at the Navy dormitory where most of the others on the team ate. Jo washed dishes and trays there in return for meals. No one explained why — Jo had been working there since he first arrived in Madison about five months before — but orders came down from a Navy official saying Jo could not work at the mess hall anymore until he got security clearance.

The coach had heard about it, and when Jo showed up for practice that evening, the coach seemed apprehensive. He finally took Jo aside and asked, "You're not mad?"

"No," Jo said. It hurt but he could do nothing about it anyway.

"I'd be mad if I were you," the coach said. "Never heard so much bull in my life. They gave me this stuff about you being Japanese, needing security clearance to wash dishes. I told them you're from California, not Japan, for Christ sakes. The stupids can't see the difference."

"Well...," Jo said, then said no more though he appreciated the coach's feeling.

"I won't bring it up again," the coach said. "I just wanted to let you know that a lot of us are on your side."

On Thursday following the team's return from Penn State, the team had had its final workout in preparation for a return match against the team from the Navy preflight school in Ottumwa. Jo had left the field house and was starting across the open football practice field toward the Ag campus when he heard Kowalski call.

"You headed my way?" the sailor asked as he caught up, puffing a bit.

"Yeah," Jo said. "Got a new job in the dining hall at the short-course farm training center."

"Good," Kowalski responded, then asked, "How do you think we'll do tomorrow night? Heard they're pretty tough."

"Hell, you'll do all right."

"Hope so. How's your weight?"

"Almost there," Jo said. "All I need to do is dry out tonight."

"I'm already down to 175," Kowalski said. "Coach even told me to eat a normal meal tonight."

The two walked in silence for a while, crunching through the crust that had formed on the patches of snow scattered over the field. Light from the street lamps shining through the barren

branches of trees caught the white vapor of their breath.

"You know, Jo, there's something I want to tell you," Kowalski said. "Did you read that stuff in the newspapers about what happened at Penn State?"

"Yeah," Jo said. "They said what the coach told us he would tell them."

"There's more to it, you know," Kowalski said.

"Oh? What?"

"You don't hear much of the scuttlebutt around the dorms or at the student union. I never see you there."

"I've gotta work," Jo said.

"We know that," Kowalski said. "I'm not criticizing. What I want to tell you, though, is what people are saying about why the coach was so mad about the decision against you at Penn State. It was the referee; what he said in the locker room before the matches when he came to your name on the list of fighters."

"Oh?"

"Yeah," Kowalski said. "Coach got mad as hell; ready to call all the bouts off. He's in the Navy, though, only a chief petty officer; would've been so easily overruled."

"What did the referee say?"

Kowalski stumbled a bit. "Don't get mad," he said. "But you know what the ref said when he saw your name? He said he wasn't going to let any 'Jap boy' win, no matter what if he could help it. Said it right in front of the coach."

"Oh," Jo said.

"Some people are like that," Kowalski said as he put his arms on Jo's shoulder. "I'm sorry."

"Hell, it's not your fault," Jo said. "Thanks for telling me."

As they walked the half moon, which had been hidden behind some clouds, came out. In the moonlight Jo could see the silhouette of the domed observatory above them on the top of the hill on the backside of the Ag campus. The white patches of snow on the darkened ground looked almost like clouds; even the observatory itself looked as if it may have been floating in the sky. It gave Jo a lonely feeling.

"Well, I turn off here," Jo said when they reached a corner.

"We'll see you," Kowalski said. "No problems?" They were under a street lamp now and could see each other's face clearly.

"None, Carl," Jo said, and suddenly realized he had used Kowalski's first name. Everybody called Kowalski "Kowalski." Nobody ever seemed to use his first name, but Jo just did, and his friend gave him a wide grin as they parted.

Chapter Eight
Sister

Dec. 17, 1944: Finally...Public Proclamation number 21 was issued. General DeWitt's mass exclusion orders were rescinded...Even in the proclamation the federal government worked to protect its political position on the West Coast by stressing the care it took before restoring the ethnic Japanese to their full rights... (Commission Report, page 235)

O

Jo would have ignored the poster, but it was posted on the wall just opposite him in the tiny passenger lounge on the top deck of the train-carrying freighter going across Lake Michigan from Milwaukee to Muskegon. The caricature of a grinning Japanese soldier with protruding teeth, large ears, horned-rimmed glasses, and a brown, cloth cap with a red star over a crinkled visor stared out from the poster. The rays of the rising sun silhouetted the smoke and ruins of a bombed city in the background. The words: "JAP...You're Next" was blazoned diagonally across the poster in bold, black lettering.

The poster was more virulent and uglier than others Jo had seen. It was a newer one. World War II was already over in Europe and the emphasis now was on the war against Japan. Jo wondered if it was by the same cartoonist who drew other posters he had seen in bus and train stations in Wyoming and Montana, on the "El" in Chicago, and the men's room at the Oscar Meyer meat plant in Madison, where he worked on weekends.

From the poster his eyes shifted to the other passengers. A little girl, about 10 or 11, wearing bobby sox, black and white oxfords, a pleated skirt and a light cardigan, sat opposite him. About his sister Kimi's age, Jo thought. How old was Kimi now anyway? Jo had left the family in camp a year and a half before. Even while in camp, he was constantly going in and out — topping sugar beets, harvesting peas, digging ditches — and had seen his family only occasionally. For three years or so he really was not around enough to watch his sister grow. His father and mother — he knew they would be all right, somehow.

Now that the reunion with his family was imminent, Jo's loneliness surfaced. He wanted to get home in a hurry.

Unconsciously, he had been staring at the little girl sitting in front of him. The girl, embarrassed, smiled weakly. Jo returned the smile, then got up and moved onto the deck into the sunshine.

The Milwaukee shoreline already had disappeared below the horizon. The water, a dark blue in the distance, was a clear bluish-green below the railing of the ship. Near the prow the water was being turned over — like soil being plowed — into furrows before foaming and merging into the wake.

Watching and waiting — the ship's movement seemed so slow. His sister, mother and father, home — he wondered what it would look like. The family could have stayed in camp a bit longer, but Father was restless. With nothing to go back to in California, his father and mother took a job offer from Holland, Michigan — $150 a month for the work of two, plus food and housing. Mother could cope with anything. How was his father adjusting? And Kimi?

The Greyhound bus station in downtown Muskegon was dark and dingy. Though the sun was still up, not much light came through into the waiting room. A film of bluish-gray covered the two rows of wooden benches, the newspaper stand, the Coke machine, the red neon light above the lunch counter. The tile floor needed mopping. Only a recruiting poster — Uncle Sam, sleeves rolled up, saying "I need YOU" — seemed new and clean.

Jo lifted his head each time the shadows blocked the sunlight coming through the open entrance of the waiting room. "Takes an hour from Holland to Muskegon," Kimi had said on the phone. "Should be there before 6 o'clock." His watch showed almost 6. The Newsweek he bought lay open on his suitcase, unread. Could be that they're going to be late.

Suddenly, someone gave his suitcase a slight kick.

"Kimi..." was all he could say. She and a little blond-haired girl had come through a side door. What a way to greet a person, Jo thought. Not even a "Hello," just a kick of a suitcase. I'm your brother, remember? he wanted to ask, but said nothing.

Before he could fully catch her eyes, Kimi turned to introduce the little blond girl — Sandy. Sandy, her tresses falling over the shoulders of her white T-shirt, was shy but smiled, genuinely happy to see him. She was the daughter, an only child, of the Hobson's, the family his mother and father worked for.

"Pa's waiting outside in the station wagon," Kimi said and began walking toward the side entrance while Jo was still picking up his raincoat and suitcase.

His father was all smiles. The hair was grayer along the fringes; the mustache almost totally white; the face was more wrinkled. He had lost weight.

Momentarily, Jo didn't know what to say. *"Itte mairi mashita"* — a Japanese phrase he had learned to say while still in kindergarten and used for years whenever he came home from school — seemed inappropriate. The formal bow and the greetings used by the older Japanese or in the scenes of the few Japanese movies he had seen, he had not really learned to do.

"Doh?" his father asked in simple Japanese, to which Jo shrugged his shoulders, then smiled. He didn't have to say anything.

"Sore wa ii," his father said. His smiling could not hide the glistening of tears in his eyes.

From Kimi's letters Jo knew that the Hobson's, though they lived on a farm, were not farmers but part owners of a small chain of drug stores. His father's job was to tend several acres of land, look after two cows, a half dozen pigs, and a flock of chickens; take care of the garden and yard around the main house, and to be a general handyman. His mother cooked and cleaned house for the Hobsons. But Jo had a lot of questions to ask.

The work is not hard, his father explained. He cultivated about four acres, growing feed corn and alfalfa for the livestock and sweet corn, string beans, lettuce, tomatoes, cucumbers and egg plants for home use. He also took care of a egg-laying chickens, raised some hogs, and grazed two cows. They got all the gasoline they needed since the Hobsons were classified as farmers and even got extra sugar for canning purposes, he said.

He said Mother got along fine with Mrs. Hobson. They had an automatic dishwasher as well as a washing machine, so it took a load off of her work. Kimi seemed to like school — only about 30 children for all six grades with two teachers and an assistant. The principal, who also teaches, made a special visit to introduce herself when she learned that a Japanese family had moved into the area and would be sending a child to her school.

"Shimpai nai," his father said. Everything would work itself out.

Jo listened and watched the countryside roll by as his father talked while he drove. No rancor or bitterness was indicated in his father's voice though he would have had to carry a heavy sense of loss over the California farm as he worked someone else's land. From what his father said, Jo could sense that his father looked on the farming he did for the Hobsons like child's play. Father did not have to worry about the costs of seeds, fertilizers or insect sprays; he could get all he needed to make things grow. Nor did he have to worry about market prices. It was amateur farming.

Occasionally Jo caught glimpses of the lake as the station wagon moved on by sand dunes on one side, wooded areas and rich farm land on the other. He couldn't resist the urge and kept looking into the rearview mirror to look at his sister's face. She didn't seem to notice as she talked and giggled with Sandy.

"The principal, *namai wa nani?*" Jo asked his father.

"*So ne...*I've forgotten; it's a Dutch name," the father said, then looked into the rearview mirror and asked Kimi in Japanese.

"Mrs. Van Dusen. She's the one with two of her own kids in school — Meg and Kevin — who come over to play sometimes," Kimi said. Her speaking English to their father bothered Jo. Though he and she never used Japanese when conversing between themselves, with Mother or Father they always used Japanese, though, of course, English words were thrown in if they did not know or had forgotten the Japanese words. Maybe Kimi was using English because of Sandy.

Sandy, who sat patiently waiting for Kimi to answer her father's question, stole a shy glance at Jo, showed warm curiosity.

Darkness had almost set in by the time they reached the farm. Even before the station wagon had come to a full stop in front of the small cottage, Jo could see his mother holding open the screen door, peering out.

"The Hobsons, *asa ni* — in the morning — you can meet them," his father said as Sandy, who mumbled a "so nice to meet you," ran off to the main house a short distance away. "See you tomorrow, Kathy," is what he thought he heard her say as she was leaving.

"*Ma-a, Jo ga kaite kitta,*" Kimi said the obvious as she scurried with the suitcase through the door ahead of Jo and his father.

"*Shibaraku,*" his mother said at the door. She wiped her hands on her apron — she always seemed in the midst of cooking or washing whenever Jo came home from anywhere — then put her hands on Jo's shoulders and blinked to clear her eyes as she looked. "*Yoku kairi mashita* — it's good you've come home."

The rice was already cooked, and as Kimi showed Jo where the bathroom was, his mother put on a hot plate for *sukiyaki*. She also had *tempura*, *sashimi*, pickled cucumbers, *takuwan* and *tofu* on the table. Jo's father immediately began warming up some *sake*.

"Drink, do you?" Mother asked in Japanese. Jo hadn't developed a taste for *sake* yet, but he'd join his father for the special occasion.

"*Bee-ru*," Jo told his mother, and only occasionally. As he watched her add bamboo shoots, *aburage* and *konyaku* to the meat and vegetables already cooking in the pan, he asked where they were able to get the Japanese foodstuff.

Before his mother or father could answer, Kimi broke in. "From the Nakano's," she said. "They're at the chick sexing center in Zeeland. They go to Chicago, to an Oriental food shop there. They always ask us what we need."

"Nice of them," Jo said. "Where are they originally from?"

"Gee, I'm not sure," Kimi said, then turning to her father, asked, "Los Angeles *no ho datta desho*."

Her speaking in Japanese to her parents was much more comfortable to listen to.

The Hobsons were in their mid-fifties. Mrs. Hobson, graying hair tied in a bun, had a thin face, well-tanned; her voice was low-pitched. But she spoke more with her eyes — large blue ones which widened and narrowed as she talked, distracting attention from her words.

Mr. Hobson showed a lot more gray in his closely-cropped hair. He wore light-colored, plastic-rimmed glasses over round, small eyes, and smoked a pipe continuously. When he smiled, his teeth showed a mixture of brown tobacco stain and shiny gold.

"So nice to meet you," Mrs. Hobson said as his father introduced him. "Your mother was so happy when she learned that you were finally coming. It's been quite some time since she last saw you, I understand. And Kathy, too; she showed Sandy the letter you wrote."

Kathy? Then he recalled his sister had said in one of her letters she was using the name "Kathy" since "Kimiko" was hard for people at school to pronounce.

"It's Saturday. I don't go to work. Sit and talk a while," Mr. Hobson said as Jo's father excused himself to do morning chores while Mrs. Hobson went to the kitchen to make some coffee.

"We're happy that your father and mother came to join us," Mr. Hobson said. "They're good workers. Your mother doesn't speak much English but she seems to understand. Has a sense of humor, always laughing. Your father does wonders with the vegetables in the garden. Never really saw anything like it — some of broccoli, peppers or tomatoes, for example, so lush. Kathy makes a good playmate for Sandy, too."

Mr. Hobson also asked about school in Madison. He had heard about the lakes in the state capital, the large campus, the La Follettes — "Quite radical, even for today."

"Went to Michigan State myself," he said, and though he was asking about Jo's school, did most of the talking.

Later, he swung the conversation back to Kathy. "Your sister, she's very independent," he said.

"Is she?" Jo asked. What was the man trying to get at.

"For example," Mr. Hobson said, "the other day Sandy wanted to play. Kathy said she was too tired, or something, didn't want to. But about fifteen minutes later, Kathy rode off on her bicycle alone. Seemed awfully unfair. The bicycle — it's one that used to be Sandy's."

"Maybe Kathy just wanted to be alone," Jo said. He could sense the indignation in the man's voice. But his sister did not have to make anyone a good playmate. She was not hired help.

"Let's go for a swim," Kathy suggested later after they had left the Hobsons. Jo was all for it. He had walked around the farm, then helped his father pick string beans and corn, feed the pigs and chickens, and hoe part of a new beans patch so his father could take the afternoon off. Jo was sweaty. More important, Jo and Kimi could talk alone.

"Sandy and I, some of the other kids, we have a favorite spot," Kimi said as she led the way along a path over the sand dunes.

"Must be nice," Jo said, then asked, "you and Sandy, you do get along?"

"Oh sure," she said, "when it's only the two of us." She said Sandy was only 10, in the fifth grade rather than the sixth so some of those in Kimi's class would get tired of waiting for her when they played games and things. "But she's fun when other kids, or her father and mother aren't around."

They trudged in silence for a while. The hurt he felt at the bus station was almost forgotten. After supper the night before she was full of things she wanted to tell him — the school, the other kids (she played third base on the boys' softball team because there weren't enough boys), the class trip to Grand Rapids, the tulip festival in town. While she talked and showed him the picture album she had started, he kept thinking he should have been around when the family moved to the area. He could have helped her.

As the two emerged from the dunes and onto the beach, they approached a woman in a broad-brimmed beach hat and swimsuit lying in the sun.

"Kathy, how are you?" the woman asked.

"Fine, thank you," the sister said.

"And your father and mother?"

"They're fine, too."

During the conversation, Jo stood only a yard or so away. He liked the woman's warmth and friendliness, and smiled awkwardly when the woman looked at him. He was about the introduce himself when his sister began moving on, and Jo moved with her.

"Who's that lady?" Jo asked after they had gone a few steps.

"Oh, that's Mrs. Van Dusen. She's the teacher who visited Mom and Pop when we first moved here."

"Why didn't you introduce me?"

"I just...I don't know."

"That's okay. Was curious, that's all," Jo said. But he wanted to shake her, get her out of her shell, have her talk to him of what was bothering her so.

For the next several days Jo could not help but take special notice of what his little sister did or said. Alone with him or with their mother and father, she seemed to be seeking a closeness. She was with him as he helped his father with the chores. She rode on the side fender of the little John Deere tractor as Jo plowed and disked a field for fall crops of broccoli, cauliflower, cabbage and lettuce. She and he went together to bring in the cows in the evening from the far side of an abandoned apple orchard where the animals grazed.

On Sunday, though, when the family went to the Presbyterian church in town, she was again aloof, lonely and lost — acted as she did in the bus depot, with Mrs. Van Dusen at the beach, as if she wanted to dissociate herself from Jo, her mother and father. She stayed in the station wagon when they visited Mr. Hobson's office at the drug firm. In the five-and-ten store, they met a mother and some children — Kimi's school mates — but she never introduced Jo.

At the end of the week, Jo's father drove him back to Muskegon for the return trip across the lake. Kimi was excited about going along — instead of the bus depot, they would go straight to the dock area. She would get a chance to see the freighter. "I'll tell you about it when I get back," Jo heard her promise Sandy, who, because of piano lessons, could not go along.

"Think they'll let me and Pa on the boat?" Kimi asked long before they reached the harbor area.

"If there's time," Jo assured her.

The station wagon pulled up by the slip for the train ferry as a locomotive was pushing the last string of freight cars into the hold of the ship.

"Sure," the guard at the gangplank said when Jo asked. "They'll blow the ship's horn when we're about ready to leave. They'll have plenty of time to get off."

The three boarded; Jo carrying his suitcase, his father the cardboard laundry box Jo was to use to send home his clothes for washing, and his sister the lunch bag his mother had packed. The other passengers had not arrived yet.

"This the boat you came across on?" Kimi asked as they stepped onto the top deck.

"It's a ship, not a boat," Jo laughed as her eyes darted over the deck. "Looks like the same one, but I don't know. The railway has several of the same type. All look alike."

"How big is it?"

"About 10,000 tons, I imagine."

"Where do the captain and the pilot stay?"

"On the bridge, over there."

"The passengers?"

"In the cabin with the glass windows at the center of the deck."

"Let's hurry then, leave your things there so we can see the rest of the ship," his sister said as she impatiently grabbed his free hand and began pulling him toward the passenger lounge.

About five yards from the cabin, his sister, tired of Jo's slower pace, let go his hand and ran ahead to the lounge. The father was now several paces back.

When Jo got to the lounge only several seconds after his sister, he could see her face through the glass. Her face was turned up toward the poster on the wall — the same poster Jo had seen earlier — but her eyes were shut tight as if she was trying to blot out the whole ugly caricature.

As Jo entered, she turned toward him, her face flushed, tears in her eyes.

"Are we like that — you and me, Ma and Pa?" she asked.

"No," Jo said. "No."

"But...but people say...Aren't we..."

"Don't worry about what people say," Jo said. He could feel her sobs as she buried her face in his shoulder. Cry, let her cry, get it out of her system.

After a quick moment, however, her sobbing stopped. As he took the lunch bag from her hand, he turned her gently toward the door.

"Wait outside for Pa," he said. "I'll put this stuff in the corner, then join you."

"Okay," she said simply, the flush and traces of emotion now gone; a curtain again drawn over her inner anxieties.

Chapter Nine
Our Farm
(Part II)

January 19, 1948: The U.S. Supreme Court reverses the ruling of the California Supreme Court in the Oyama v. California case, ruling a key provision of the state's Alien Land Law unconstitutional.

April 17, 1952: The California State Supreme Court rules the Alien Land Law unconstitutional by a 4-3 vote. (Fujii Sei V. State of California).

O

Seven years after the family had left their California home WWII already had ended, but Jo was in the U.S. Army, on leave visiting his mother and father in New York. His leave was about over and he was to start the next day for his new post at the Army Language School in Monterey. His mother and father were working as domestics for a family on Park Avenue. They had been back in their apartment for the weekend, but now were to return to the Park Avenue home where his mother was the cook, and his father, the butler and all around handy man.

At the door where they were saying goodbye, Jo searched his mother's face. More signs of tiredness showed around her eyes; her hair, still done in a bun, was grayer. She had aged and Jo was worried. When he asked about the work, she had assured him it was not too strenuous, though his father had said Mrs. Kahn, the mother of the family they worked for, had a never ending flow of guests.

"Don't forget," his mother said just before she turned. She wanted him to visit the Nakano's and some of the other families who had returned to the San Francisco Bay Area after the war. Mrs. Nakano had asked about him in her letters when she learned that he was at Fort Ord for his basic training. Jo was the first of his family to have returned to California since the evacuation.

"*Shimpai nai,*" Jo assured her for at least the fifth time. The Army Language School was at the Presidio in Monterey, not far from Mountain View, and he would visit the Nakano's as soon as he got the chance.

"If you have time," his father said simply. With that his father took the small carrier bag Jo had taken to the door for him and bade him goodbye.

Jo watched his mother and father walk down the foyer into the sunlight. His mother still wore the same dark silk dress she had in camp and before; his father, maybe the same gray suit. Take a cab back to work, Jo had suggested, but no, his father said, the subway stop was only two blocks from the Kahn's home.

Back in the living room Jo sat on the worn couch and went over what he had to do. He'd hitch a ride out of Mitchell Field. With any luck he'd be in Monterey with time to spare.

He looked around the room; the Army surplus cot, the cardboard moveable closet, the folding chairs, a card table — everything seemed temporary. Home was where his parents were, and for such a long time, ten years or so, each time he managed to get home, home was in a different place: the "relocation center" in Wyoming, the farmhand's cottage in Michigan, the servants' room at the Weiss' in Glen Cove. At least now his parents had an apartment they could return to.

When Jo had first arrived in the apartment at the start of his leave, he immediately recognized the hollowed piece of gray granite, a miniature Indian grindstone about the size of a man's open hand that was placed on a walnut-stained stand next to a wall mirror. A flint arrowhead, almost perfectly shaped, was next to the grindstone. His father had found the grindstone (Jo often wondered how many ages ago it might have actually been used) in their pea patch; Jo the arrowhead while irrigating. The two pieces of stone were the only reminders of the farm in California.

During his stay, neither his father nor mother ever mentioned the farm. In fact Jo could not remember either of them ever mentioning the farm over all the years since the evacuation.

Jo had already left the Wyoming camp by the time the farm had to be sold and only learned of what had happened in a letter from his brother. Jo could only guess at what his parents' feelings were over the loss; he never heard even a hint of any bitterness or self-pity.

Jo's father did the grocery shopping for the Kahn family. There were two vegetable and fruit stands off of Fifth Avenue, where Jo's father went several times a week. Jo had watched his father shop. His father would feel a cantelope for its ripeness, snap the string beans to test for freshness, study a cauliflower for its whiteness, look at the celery stalks to see if they had been properly bleached.

Whenever Jo passed a fruit and vegetable, the produce on display would remind him of what they grew and had on the farm. His father's shopping chore, Jo felt, had to be almost a daily reminder of what was once almost theirs.

Jo wondered — how do people learn to accept the loss of a life-time dream?

O

Jo could have visited the old farm much earlier. He had been back in California for almost two months, had visited the Nakano's and other family friends. But he stayed away from the farm. Was he afraid — like removing the scab from a wound before it had healed? He wasn't sure. Being so close, however, he remained curious about seeing his old home.

A photo Mrs. Nakano showed him during his last visit — a snapshot taken during a joint family picnic — sparked his decision. They held the picnics under an old live oak tree with branches broad and flat enough to walk on. While studying the picture, he decided to borrow a camera and take some shots, let his parents see what the place was like now.

Most of what he saw as he drove down the Bayshore Highway, now eight rather than four lanes, was new — the houses, a low modernistic office building, a fiber glass plant. The scrub shrubbery along the highway, an occasional orchard or an alfalfa field looked familiar. But when he looked up at the brown, dry foothills northeast of the valley and the dark blue mountains silhouetted in the background, the past came sharply into focus, especially that December day when he, on the back of the pickup with his brother, saw the farm for the first time.

Once past the huge silver hanger at Moffet Field, his pulse quickened. He should be able to see the eucalyptus grove soon. When the trees came into view, he strained to see further ahead — he should be sighting the barn and the pine trees, then the house and the windmill. But he saw no barn, no pine tree, no house; only the windmill, which had half its blades missing.

"Used to live on the farm," Jo explained to the woman who answered the door at a new house built just off the paved road near the start of the dirt drive onto the farm. "Would you mind? I'd like to look around."

Because of the sun behind him, he couldn't see her face very clearly through the screen door. She fussed a bit with her hair, then reached for the lock on the screen door; so she could open it, he thought, but then realized she was just making sure it was locked.

"Well, I suppose it'd be all right," the woman said. "My husband Frank should be home soon. I'll tell him you're here."

"Thanks," Jo said, though the tone of her voice wasn't friendly. Belli, who owned a small trucking business, used to haul the produce from the farm to the San Francisco wholesale market. When Jo's family and their neighbors had to leave the farm, Belli was to look after the farm until the families returned. Jo didn't know what the arrangements were, but had been told that Belli had become the owner of the farm.

Driving down the old dirt road, Jo saw little that was familiar. Sugar beets had replaced the walnut trees. The cows next door were gone, the dairy barn replaced by a corrugated sheet- tin hanger with two small spray airplanes parked in front. Ahead of him, though, he could see the valley oaks where the garage had been.

Jo stopped the car under one of the large oaks, turned off the motor, then sat and looked. Only part of the old house remained. A battered front door, broken and boarded windows, and milkweed and nettles a foot or so high in the garden. To the rear he could see a stump where one of the pine trees stood. Where the other pine and the barn used to be was now part of the sugar beet field.

When he saw the petrified log in what used to be his father's rock garden, he left the car and made his way through the weeds to the log despite the burrs and foxtails he would get on his socks and pants legs. Though the stump it was originally leaned against was gone, the log remained partly upright. He examined it a while — most of the crystallized carbon had fallen off — then sat on it and ran his hands over the smooth surface, its hard smoothness reminding him of sharpening stones used on beet knives and other farm tools.

The flowering cherry, peach, apricot and plum trees the family had planted or grafted were taller now, but all had spiny boughs on their unattended branches. He looked up at the windmill. Half its wind blades were missing, its wooden tank was eroded, dry rot had eaten through the bottom boards.

Jo sat on the log for uncounted minutes. The buzzing of a bumblebee and the chirping of a sparrow could be heard above the silence. A white cabbage butterfly flitted by. A bee fly lit on the tiny purple flowers of a nearby milkweed. With a quick, short sweep, he caught the fly, held it a moment, then smiled as he let it go. It looked like a honey bee, though it was fatter, a shade darker brown and shinier — details his father had originally pointed out to him. He used to fool his playmates by catching bee flies in his hands while they watched in awe, wondering why he never got stung.

In the silence, Jo recalled his mother's face that day when she was having her last look at their home and his own jumbled emotions as he watched.

They had been told then that going to the camps would be their contribution to the war effort; though with the country at war, maybe no reason was really needed. As he thought of his mother, Jo's stomach muscles tightened; then the tightness moved up through his chest and then to his throat muscles.

He wanted to shout his protest.

Who were these people who so arbitrarily judged his mother and father untrustworthy and took away their home and their livelihood? Roosevelt... Warren ...? Two he always held in high regard. General DeWitt? The U.S. Military? The American Legion? The Daughters of the Golden West? His anger over the arrogance and bigotry cried out in his mind.

Later, driving away from the farm, as Jo's ire cooled, he felt relieved. Over the years he had had lingering doubts that the evacuation might have had some legitimacy. The burst of anger, however, cleared all such doubts. It was like removing his field pack after a long march, one so long he had half forgotten he had its weight on his back.

He had no reason to think about the farm anymore. The camera he had borrowed for his visit to the farm remained untouched.

Chapter Ten
A Soldier Is a Soldier

June 25, 1950: North Korea invades South Korea. The United States was convinced that the Korean War made an early peace treaty with Japan imperative... President Truman announced in mid-September, 1950, that the United States intended to begin informal discussions with the Allies on the question. (Hugh Borton, Japan's Modern Century, the Ronald Press Company, New York, August, 1955, page 436.)

O

Jo studied the other passengers on the bus. Could any of them be a relative? The farm woman in baggy, unbleached denim workpants, a pin-striped blue blouse and a graying bonnet — could she be a cousin? The heavy-set man with white whiskers and an unlit pipe in his mouth might be an uncle. A woman in the dark purple kimono with a girl maybe six, the five girls in navy blue school uniforms — another cousin, nieces? It was silly, he knew. A chance meeting of a relative on the bus? Practically nil. But the closer he got to Hachiman, the more his curiosity grew, and his mind kept feeding on any possibility, no matter how remote.

It was late Fall, 1950. Jo had taken the night train from Tokyo to Gifu, riding in one of the first-class coaches reserved for Allied Occupation personnel. But now he was on a regular bus with the Japanese on his way to Hachiman, a town deep in the southern Japan Alps. From there he was to go to his father's native village, still further into the mountains.

Jo had never met any relatives outside his immediate family. He did not know what the relatives he might look like, nor did he even know how many there were.

The visit to his father's native village was one his parents in New York were especially anxious for him to make, he being the first of the family to return to Japan after more than 25 years.

He had arrived in Japan three months earlier, shipping out of the U.S Army depot in Oakland the day the Korean War started. Luckily, he was assigned to the Translators and Interpreters Service at GHQ in Tokyo instead of being sent immediately to Korea as were most of the others on board the troopship, the General Pope.

The bus stopped at a small countryside store to pick up a woman in farmer's clothes and her five or six-year-old son. As the two were making their way to an empty seat a few rows in front of Jo, the little boy yanked on his mother's sleeve, "*Mama. Mama. Heitai-san* — a soldier," he said.

"Sh...," the mother said, as Jo looked up. She smiled her apology, then put her arm around the boy's shoulder to turn him so he would face the front.

It's okay, Jo indicated with a smile. But he suddenly was aware that everyone on the bus was looking his way; even the bus driver glanced up into his rear view mirror.

The sudden attention brought into sharp focus what was at the core of Jo's emotions since his arrival in Japan. Japanese American? American Japanese? Born in Tokyo, raised in America since he was a six months old, now back in Japan as an American GI, speaking only elementary Japanese but still legally a Japanese national since, even as a soldier, U.S. laws barred him from U.S. citizenship — Jo wondered what others thought.

"The Japanese — how do they see you? As a renegade? A traitor, even?" Barfield, his first sergeant, kiddingly asked when Jo went to pick up his leave papers.

"Shit no."

He was PFC Joji Kono, an American GI with the U.S. Occupation Forces in Japan.

Maybe it was the newness of his experience, maybe just the atmosphere of the Occupation. Anyway, what he found most galling since his arrival in Japan was the theme — repeated over and over during orientation, in training classes, during briefings and in pamphlets, that they, the Americans, were there to teach the Japanese democracy, and the air of superiority the theme engendered among some of the Occupation personnel. He wondered if they were so naive as to think the Japanese weren't aware of America's anti-Asian laws on immigration and citizenship, or housing, for examples, or the segregation of blacks in America's South?

At home, Jo could live with the situation; things could be changed. In Japan, however ... The hell with it, he thought, but a bitterness he didn't want to admit to remained in the pit of his stomach.

As the bus chugged up and around sharp curves, occasionally pulling off to the side of the road to let an on-coming truck or car by, Jo caught glimpses of the morning sun reflected off of a stream a hundred feet or so below. Paddy fields flanked by thatched-roofed farm houses and sheds seemed carved out of mountain sides. Men and women with conical straw hats could be seen bent over their tasks. Jo could feel an urge — one he felt from the day of his arrival in Japan — to be one of them; to toil and sweat, feel what they felt. How else could he understand being Japanese?

Two hours later — the road's ascent seemed endless — the bus finally moved into a small valley. To one side, narrow-gauged railway cars, which looked like toys when compared to the freight cars at home, stood intermixed with flat-bottom gondolas, some stacked with lumber, others empty. In a far corner lay twisted rails, other debris, and the stubbed remains of a steel radio transmission tower.

However, no signs of the war could be seen as the bus moved through the main street of a town. Small shops, like those in Tokyo's suburbs, lined both sides of the street. But unlike Tokyo, the air was clean. The vermilion trimmings of storefronts with shiny black and orange finishes, the show windows, the brown and red roof tiling, even the unpainted wood of the buildings, looked newly washed. Instead of gutters, water seemingly clean enough to drink flowed in stone flues along each side of the street. Here and there rice bowls, chopsticks, dishes, pots and pans were drying on trays at the water's edge.

On his left, through the openings between shops and low buildings, he caught glimpses of a swiftly-flowing river, its white wake highlighted by the water's blue and light green.

Beyond the river, dark, tree-covered mountains rose steeply. Jo pressed his face against the bus window for a glance at the mountain peaks.

Small wonder that his father was such a nature lover, Jo thought as the bus slowed to a stop. Then to his delight, he saw a white wooden sign with black military lettering (also the only reminder he could see of the Occupation) which read "Hachiman," both in Roman letters and *Kanji*.

"*Erashai-mase,*" a man in his mid-twenties, about Jo's age, said as he bowed when Jo stepped off of the bus. It was Isamu, the cousin Jo had sent the letter to so the relatives knew he was coming.

"*Hajima mashite,*" Jo said, returning the man's bow. Isamu, thin and a bit taller than Jo, had his black hair neatly combed back, giving emphasis to a sharp nose and pointed features. He had on a worn, though neatly pressed, gray suit and a woven tie, making Jo suddenly conscious of his crumpled, olive-drab uniform.

Before Jo had a chance to study his cousin's face — Jo didn't see any family resemblance — two women and a man in kimono, and a second man in a western-style suit moved forward.

Through the bowing and exchange of greetings, Jo didn't catch any of the names, but each was a cousin, aunt or uncle. Meeting five at once left him more confused than acquainted.

Isamu, who had taken a day off from his job with the county government, and Miyoko, a cousin, took Jo to an inn just a few doors away, where Jo could freshen up, have lunch and then go over the schedule that had been planned for him. The others, bowing their apologies, left to return to work. Except for Isamu, all of them obviously were older than Jo, and Jo felt a tinge of embarrassment — maybe he should have been bowing to them first rather than the other way around.

At the inn, Jo and Isamu were comfortably seated by a hibachi in a balcony-like room which extended over the river. Miyoko, whose husband owned the inn, had gone to order the lunch.

Leaning back and smiling, Isamu explained how relieved he was that Jo spoke some Japanese. The letter that Jo had sent ahead of his visit had been written by a Japanese where Jo worked. Isamu wasn't sure if Jo spoke any Japanese at all, since he had heard that many Nisei did not speak the language, and nobody in town could really speak that much English.

Studied it at the Army language school, Jo said, though he still had problems reading and writing Japanese.

By custom, Jo was to spend the first night at the *hon-ke* — the ancestral home, Isamu said as he went over a schedule that had been planned for Jo. He said it was the house Jo's father was born in. Isamu, his wife and their two children now lived there with Jo's oldest uncle, the family patriarch. The home was in a village about 12 miles further into the mountains, and after lunch, Isamu would take Jo there on his mo-ped. Jo would spend the second night at the home of another uncle, the one closest to Jo's father's age. On Saturday, Isamu said, all of Jo's relatives — Jo's father was the youngest of seven children — would gather back in Hachiman to meet him.

As Isamu talked, Jo could hardly keep from looking out over the scenery. With the *shoji* pulled aside, a panorama of the mountains and stream was spread before them. Some trees along the banks of the river — the *Nagara-gawa* — were showing yellow and red, though the dark green of pine and cypress trees remained dominant.

Above the river, about two-thirds of the way up what seemed the highest peak of the nearby mountains, Jo could see a castle, its eaves turned skyward, its white paint and gray granite gleaming in the sun.

Isamu said the castle, built in the mid-1600's, was a favorite landmark for people of the area. With what could have been a painful smile, he said that during the war it was a focal point in the flight pattern for the American B-29 bombers. The planes flew in from over Nagoya, then would turn right above the castle towards targets further to the northeast. The bombers, he said, followed the same route through the mountains that typhoons did.

Miyoko, when she returned, had dozens of anecdotes to tell about Jo's father when the father was young. Jo's father was able to catch the elusive *ayu* — a trout like fish — with his bare hands in the mountain streams and was always in the mountains, hunting or fishing, she said. He never seemed to study, but did well in school and was one of the few from the village to leave to go to high school, she said. He was always a dreamer, as well, she said: used to play games about traveling the world. No one was really surprised when he ended up living overseas.

She reminded Jo of his own oldest sister — flat nose, the fold of her eyelids, a round face.

O

The flat wooden deck of the river ferry was small. Jo, his duffle bag and small back pack, and Isamu and his mo-ped, took up a third of the deck space. Two steel cables, anchored on both banks of the river, straddled the ferry while a third was attached to a two-cylinder motor, which popped and smoked as it was revved up. The ferryman, in an old pair of denim coveralls and wearing a conical straw hat, could have been as old as the ferry itself. He was lean, tall for a Japanese, and had a stubby white beard and a face with wrinkles running through weathered, tan skin. His arms, probably from his daily tugging on the ropes of the ferry, were sinewy.

"Ah, *Kisa no ko* — Kisa's son," he said with a smile when Isamu introduced Jo. The ferryman said he remembered Jo's father well; ferried him across the river more times than he could remember. Looking into Jo's face, he said he could see some resemblance, but that Jo had his mother's eyes. As he talked, he seemed to be reminiscing — "*Mukashi, mukashi* ... a long, long time ago...," he said without finishing his sentence.

As the ferry moved ahead, Isamu pointed across the river to a group of houses stretched along a narrow strip of land above the river bank. The houses were nestled just below the start of mountains among patches of cultivated land, thickets and ravines, and then low ridges.

The sky, by now, had turned overcast. As the wind, in gusts, blew droplets of water onto his face, Jo recalled stories his father used to tell of trapping pheasants in nets strung along probably those same ridges. The pheasants, his father said, would not fly up into the twilight air for fear of hawks. As a boy he would run through the fields, chasing the birds up the ridges into the nets. The dull whitewash of the walls of houses, the thatched roofs and the cluster of trees made Jo wonder how much may have changed from when his father had lived in the village so many years before.

On the opposite bank, the ferryman, after securing the ferry to the wooden landing dock, turned, gave Jo a quick, overall look, then said with a final nod, *"Shikkari shite* — keep your chin up."

"Arigato," Jo said. The words of support the ferryman used probably were the same words the man used when he had bid goodbye to the local youths who had gone off during the war to fight Americans.

Once off the ferry, Jo and Isamu rode the mo-ped down a narrow gravel road; Jo sitting piggy back with his baggage. People were still out in the fields and exchanged waves or nods with Isamu as the mo-ped went by. Most were either cousins or related in some way to the family, Isamu said. Jo would get a chance to meet them later.

As they approached a farm woman walking beside the road, Isamu stopped. When the woman turned, Jo was surprised. From behind he thought he saw the walk of an older woman. But beneath her bonnet, the eyes were alert, moved quickly; the face, though ruddy, was still young.

"Ara," she said, also surprised. *"Isamu."* This was a week day. Shouldn't he still be at work? He was an office supervisor and usually came home much later in the evenings, she teased.

"Jodan iu-na — stop joking," Isamu laughed, then introduced Jo. She was also a cousin.

"Ah, *yokatta*," she said, her face beaming. At last, she said, she was able to thank someone from Jo's family personally for the food packages and clothing they had sent over when the war ended. No one, she said, could ever fully appreciate how grateful she and her son felt.

"Mi-te," she said, turning up the front part of her cotton jacket to show the sweater underneath. Jo immediately recognized the beige color and stitch pattern; the cardigan was one his mother had knitted years ago and had worn around the house.

Though the cousin's enthusiasm seemed to bubble, the harsh meagerness of her life was apparent. Her teeth were still fairly white, but her gums were an off-color pink, probably from some lack in her diet. Her face was wind-burned; her hands were rough; the fingernails curved in, their cuticles cracked.

As she noticed Jo look, she stepped back slightly. *"Konna kakko* — my appearance, please forgive me," she said. She said she had to be out in the field a lot with only herself and her son, a 10-year-old, to tend to their rice paddies. Her husband, she said simply, never came back from the war. When she mentioned her husband, she paused, seemed to notice Jo's uniform for the first time.

"Gommen nasai," she said suddenly, bringing her right hand to her mouth as if she had said something wrong — maybe for mentioning the war.

Why? Why should she be apologizing, Jo wanted to ask. He searched his mind for the proper words in Japanese to express his feelings, offer condolence; could find none, and before he could say anything, the moment had passed. Her face, again smiling, hid her emotions as she turned and trudged off to a nearby field even though it was starting to get dark.

The *hon-ke* (family home) stood on a rise at the start of a small vale. In the twilight, Jo could make out rice paddies; flat rows of vines, probably yams; hedgelike rows of tea plants, and low fruit trees on the side. Close up, the house seemed much larger than it had when he and Isamu saw it from the river ferry. The thatched roof was about two feet thick. In spots where the mortar had chipped off of the outside wall, Jo could see bricks made of clayey dirt and straw. Attached to the house was a lean-to shed, where, Isamu said, they kept two sheep.

Isamu's wife Hiroko — another cousin — smiled broadly as she came out of the house, followed by her two children, a boy about four and a girl a year or so older. A circular cotton cap, typically worn by Japanese housewives, offset her round, smiling face as she bowed. Then, turning to her young son, said, *"Hiroshi, kare ga* — he's the American soldier."

The boy stepped forward, bowed quickly, then moved behind his mother, hiding his face in her apron. As the daughter stepped forward and bowed, Hiroko laughed. Her son had been asking all week who or what a *"Beigun no heitai* — an American Army soldier" was. Seeing Jo probably left him more confused than ever, she said, since Jo looked the same as any Japanese.

Once inside the house, Jo and Isamu sat on opposite sides of a quilt-covered hibachi in a sunken square hollow in the center of the main room. The room itself seemed large since its only other furniture was a floor screen partitioning the room. Hiroko, after getting some tea, went to the kitchen to prepare supper. Through the passageway Jo could see two pots and a cast iron kettle hung over an open fire. The children went to a side room to play.

"Uncle will be so glad to see you," Isamu said as they sat. "It's been such a long wait for him." He said that the old man was taking a nap so he would feel fresh when Jo arrived but would be up soon.

"Those who knew your father worried about your family when the war started," Isamu said. "But Uncle worried the most. As the family patriarch, he felt responsible for your family's well-being."

He said that early in the war when the newspapers in Japan reported that the U.S. government was rounding up the Japanese in America and putting them into concentration camps, Uncle became especially concerned.

"Uncle even sent a letter through the Red Cross...never got a response, so worried more," Isamu said.

Later, when the B-29s came flying over, there were other things to worry about, Isamu said, though even then, Uncle often expressed his concern about Jo's family. Uncle's concern over Jo's family eased somewhat only when the war was over and letters and CARE packages from Jo's father began to arrive.

"*Shikashi, kuro shitta* ... still, your family must have suffered hardship; no?" Isamu asked.

"*Maa*...well, not that much," Jo said, surprised. It was the first time anyone in Japan had asked him about the wartime evacuation of Japanese Americans from the U.S. West Coast; that anyone in Japan had expressed any concern to him over what had happened to those of Japanese ancestry in America during the war.

Jo's feelings at the time of the evacuation were muted. He was in his late teens and had never been out of California. His parents were about to lose everything — home, livelihood, and even dreams of the future for their children. But for Jo it was different. He felt no mental anguish. The very laws which barred Jo and his parents from the rights and protection of U.S. citizenship insulated Jo from the sense of betrayal felt by Nisei who were citizens. He was, after all, technically a Japanese subject and with the war, he expected even fewer rights than before.

As he recalled the evacuation — the hot sun at the race track in Santa Anita, the smell of the horse stables they were housed in, the soot in the turn-of-the century passenger cars of the train that took the internees to the camp in Wyoming — Jo looked back at his cousin and wondered what to say.

Tell him about the physical hardship? On their farm in California Jo, even while in grade school, had worked on cold spring or autumn mornings before changing clothes and rushing off to get to class in time. He had dug irrigation ditches, thinned long rows of lettuce, chopped wood, often stayed up all night in the summer time to irrigate parched fields. Physically, being in the camps was no hardship. Besides, he could not by any stretch of his imagination compare his own experiences during the evacuation with the sufferings of so many millions in the war-torn areas of the world.

But for Jo the hurt was far more than physical. He was now part of the Allied Occupation and its highly publicized goal to nurture democracy in Japan. How was he to explain to his Japanese cousin that he, Jo, a U.S. soldier whose only home was in America, could not become a U.S. citizen? Jo wondered what his cousin might see. Shame? Humiliation? That he, Jo, despite America's talk of ideals, was living a lie?

"Uncle is old and often forgets things," Isamu said, changing the subject with Jo's silence. "Because of all the anxiety caused by the war, unless Uncle can see things for himself, he won't always believe what he's been told. Often he is very depressed. Your visit will certainly help lift his spirits, ease some of the pain."

"If so, I'm glad," Jo said, though unsure of what Isamu meant by easing Uncle's "pain."

From the start, Isamu had been referring to the head of the household as *Oji-san* — Uncle — instead of using the Japanese word "*Oto-san*" or the more familiar "*Chi-chi*" for father. "I'm really his nephew," Isamu explained. "My real father is the next oldest son in the family."

He was about to say more, when a rustling sound came through the shoji from an adjacent room.

"*Ara*. Seems like Uncle's awake," Isamu said, "*Chotto gomen ...*" and got up, saying he would help the old man dress. *Oji-san*, he said, was so anxious to see Jo he would not want to waste even a minute.

As he sat alone, Jo scanned the room. In the dim light of the room's lone bulb, he could see a scroll with Chinese calligraphy in the room's alcove with the Japanese word "*Manzoku* — fulfillment." A rural work scene was painted on the screen which partitioned the room; the house's rough-hewn center beam — more than a foot and a half square — was covered with a dark stain, maybe from the soot of the open fire in the kitchen area.

As his eyes wandered, Jo wondered what his own life would have been like had his father not left the village. He could see himself toiling in the rice paddies; pulling carp from the pool in the yard Isamu and his family kept stocked; trudging up a mountain path to hunt wild boars, pheasants and other game, even bears, which seemed to abound in the region.

Then, too, with the war..., Jo was thinking, when Isamu came out from behind a screen with his uncle leaning on his right arm.

Jo got up from the *hibachi* immediately.

For a moment Jo and his uncle looked at each other. The old man's eyes, deep-set, first registered some confusion, then filled briefly with tears as Isamu gently lowered the old man to the *tatami*. Once lowered, the man got on his hands and knees and bowed. Jo did the same.

"*O kaeri-nasai*...welcome home," the old man said, then, with his head moving up and down, continued with further words of formal greeting.

Jo, his head bowing in unison with his uncle's, just mumbled — the words didn't really seem to matter. As the old man bowed, his head wavered. His cheeks were squeezed in because of a lack of teeth; the bone structure of his face was sharply outlined through thinning flesh; his face protruded; the head was bald. Jo could see no family resemblance with his father.

When the initial greetings were over, Jo stood up and helped his uncle get seated comfortably at the hibachi; Jo taking one arm, Isamu the other. Through the cotton-filled housecoat, Jo could feel the frailness of his uncle's body; smell camphor.

Once seated, his uncle studied Jo's face. Like a blind man's touch, his uncle seemed to want to extract more than what his sight would allow.

"*Yatto* … at last," the uncle said. "It's been so long. Just let me sit and look at you; feel your presence."

The old man then closed his eyelids, place his palms together in prayer, chanting "*namu ami dabutsu*" three times to give thanks to Buddha. Then, with his eyes still closed, he continued his prayer in silence.

As they waited for the old man to finish, Isamu looked over at Jo to continue their earlier conversation. Uncle, he said, had no surviving children. Since Isamu's real father had two sons, he, Isamu, was adopted by Uncle to keep the *hon-ke* under the family name.

"He had children, then?" Jo asked.

"One," Isamu said. "He was a..." Isamu began, when Uncle, who, though his eyes had been closed, had been listening, cleared his throat.

"*Hei-tai*," the old man said, then went on, "A soldier is a soldier. Some had to die. When a soldier dies..."

The old man's voice broke before he could finish, and he began to cry, tears in large droplets running down both cheeks.

"It's his age and because of Masaru," Isamu said.

"Masaru?" Jo asked.

"Umm...," Isamu nodded, then explained Masaru was Uncle's only child. "For me, he was like an older brother."

Everyone had so much hope for him, Isamu continued. Masaru did well in school, excelled at both *judo* and *kendo*, was always level-headed, and was well-liked. He eventually was to succeed Uncle as the family patriarch. They got one letter from him after his last home leave, Isamu said. Masaru spoke of hardship but, of course, could not say where he was because that was a military secret..

"When the B-29s started coming over every day, we were all afraid because the military was preparing everyone, even women, for a final stand against the Americans," Isamu said. "But we also knew that the war had to be over soon. When the Emperor announced the surrender, many were glad. Though we had not heard from Masaru for some time, we all were waiting for his return."

Jo could see Isamu struggling to control his emotions as he talked.

"For months, nothing official came," Isamu said. "Somehow, we all had assumed he would be coming home, he mattered so much to the family. Finally official word did come. He was missing in action, presumed dead. Because they never recovered his body, some still can not give up hope."

"Kino doku deshita — how unfortunate," Jo said as Isamu finished. That was all Jo could say. He didn't know; hadn't been told by his mother or father about Masaru; maybe they didn't know either.

In the silence that followed, Jo looked, first at his uncle — the old man's eyes were closed, the tear streaks on his face broken by wrinkles — and then at Isamu, whose face was now deadpan; his moist eyes avoiding contact. Jo wanted to share in their sorrow. But Masaru? Until his visit, Jo had not even known of Masaru's existence.

His uncle broke the silence.

"Ima ma de — until now..." he said, he could not accept what he had been told. Though reason told him otherwise, he said, his soul kept hoping that somehow, maybe through some miracle, his son Masaru was alive and would come home.

"Gomen — pardon my crying," he said. He said he could not help himself, that when Isamu helped him into the room, he was taken aback. His eyesight is weak and he knew it could not be, but for a moment, when he saw Jo sitting there — the uniform, Jo's youth — he thought he saw Masaru.

With that, the old man again closed his eyes as he repeated *"Namu ami dabutsu"* in prayer.

Isamu, his composure recovered, leaned toward Jo to whisper, when the old man held up his hand. The old man had more to say. He sat up straighter, turned first to Jo, then to Isamu.

"Isamu," he said, "so there'll be no mistake, please explain to Jo in simpler Japanese if Jo does not understand." He would speak slowly.

He paused, looked at the lone stripe on Jo's sleeve, then at the brass insignias on each lapel of Jo's uniform. His eyes were clear now, free of tears.

"Before I go on," he said, "I want to be sure you understand how I feel about you. You are my youngest brother's son, thus part of our family. But you are also an American, and as a soldier, *Beigun* — the American Army — is the only army you should be in."

Then he went on. *"Dai To-A Senso* — the Great East Asian War," he said, was a disaster for Japan and for the Kono family. "It had to be a tragedy, too, for the families of the Americans who died. The grief remains. For an old man like me, wishful thinking some times replaces reality, especially after wishing so hard for so long."

He paused, blinked, then added, "However, your visit to the family's ancestral home is like the return of a lost one," he continued. *"Naze*... why? I don't know. But somehow, thanks to your visit, I now feel better able to face up to the reality that my son, Masaru, is dead. May his soul rest in peace."

The old man then again prayed silently. In the silence Jo was conscious of Hiroko moving about in the kitchen area humming; the children in the other room playing and giggling; the warmth of the hibachi on his legs; the chill of the night air on his back. What ran through his mind, though, was what Sgt. Barfield has asked, "...a renegade? A traitor, even?" and his own annoyed reaction; the quizzical looks of the people on the bus; the quick glance of the river ferryman as he and Isamu left the ferry; the embarrassment and sadness showing on his widowed cousin's face when she mentioned the loss of her husband.

An American Japanese? A Japanese American? As Jo sat, it occurred to him that he could be one or the other, or both. But it no longer seemed to matter.

Chapter Eleven
Plaster Mermaid

"To many Americans they remain 'Japanese.' And in Japan some of my (Nisei) friends have been treated as 'inferior' Japanese – scorned as Koreans and Okinawans have been over the centuries…" Lynn Crost, Honor by Fire, Presidio Press, 1994, page 310.

O

In the mid-morning sunlight of a Sunday in late August, 1950, the square and the streets in front of the Shimbashi station in downtown Tokyo was empty, and, for a moment, Jo thought he may have gotten off at the wrong stop or used the wrong exit.

He was used to seeing the square in front of the station entrance only at night. As he left the exit, he saw no sign of the peddlers who would crowd the square later during the day and into the night with their assorted wares — black market American cigarettes; GI socks, shoes and underwear; Eighth Army shoulder patches; candy, sugar, toilet soap and coffee, all from the PX, and Japanese costume jewelry, plastic toys, wooden *kokeshi* dolls and even kimono with brightly colored *obi* and dainty red *geta* and slippers.

The mobile noodle stands were absent. The blended aroma of soy sauce-marinated bits of chicken, pork, beef and shrimp dripping over hot charcoal was missing. The "*Basha* — Horse Carriage," a half Westernized bar, was hardly recognizable with wooden *amado* — rain doors — covering its wide glass windows. The quiet coming and going of few weekend passers-by replaced the blare of the loudspeakers which nightly played the latest popular Japanese and American songs — "China Night" as sung by Japanese movie star Shirley Yamaguchi was still the most popular song among both the Japanese and Allied Occupation personnel.

It was only when he saw the plaster of paris mermaid in front of the "Oasis," an "on-limit" taxi dance hall where he and his fellow Nisei and other GIs went on Saturday nights, that he regained his bearings. In the sunlight the mermaid, without the soft glow of yellow, blue and orange neon lights which bathed it at night, could be seen for what it was — a shabby bit of plaster of paris, the pink and rouge paint on its face flaking, the pastel blue-green of its scaled torso faded.

Jo was still new in Japan, having arrived just two months earlier in Yokohama aboard the troopship "General Pope." (Luckily for him, though most of the 1,500 or so troops on board were immediately put on board trains after they had disembarked, sent down to the replacement depot in Sasebo and then shipped to Pusan and the fighting in Korea, while he and about two dozens others assigned to GHQ in Tokyo were kept there. He wasn't to be sent to Korea until a year later.)

This Sunday, he was on his way to visit the Kramers who were working as DACs (Department of Amery Civilians). After getting off at the Shimbashi station, Jo reread the directions in his address book – turn off the main street by a tobacco stand, follow the dirt road, make a right... He soon realized he was lost and about to return to the corner when he noticed a young woman approaching from the opposite direction.

"*Gomen nasai...*," Jo said in his politest Japanese as she came near. But the woman, in a Western-style, light beige suit and a matching pill-box hat, did not stop. Instead, her face turned red and she started walking faster, ignoring Jo.

"*Anone...*," Jo said a bit louder and started to cross the unpaved, narrow street so he might be heard easier. Then, to his surprise, the woman began to run.

Damn it, all he wanted to do was ask her if she knew where the Kramers lived. There couldn't be more than one or two Caucasian Occupation families living in the area — almost anyone from the neighborhood would know about them.

As the young woman, now walking, turned onto the main street, Jo shrugged. He, PFC Joji Kono, U.S. Army — what sort of monster did she think he was? Was it his American uniform? That he was a soldier? Or, worse yet, a Nisei soldier?

Back at the corner, Jo went to the glass-enclosed tobacco stand. "*Gai-jin no kata. Shinchu-gun* — a foreign family, with the Occupation?" he asked. The woman knew immediately.

"*Anata dake dewa nai* – it's not just you," she said. "Happens all the time with you Americans. Japan is not as large a country as yours. Distances here in Tokyo are short. Go back the way you came, but don't go quite as far. Look carefully, the turnoff is half hidden by bushes."

As she spoke, slowly and deliberately, using elementary Japanese, there was a playfulness in her voice. Jo, despite his Army language school training, still spoke Japanese with a foreign accent.

"*Arigato,*" Jo said, and the woman, round and ruddy-faced, bowed, her clean white apron crinkling over her plump body as she did so.

"*Do itashi-mashite* – Don't mention it," she said, again smiling broadly.

Jo returned her smile. He could laugh with her at his accent.

Following the tobacco woman's directions, Jo found the house quite easily. Beyond the bushes he saw a high, old cement wall with vines and beyond that, a cedar tree, two pines and an oak — all of which showed that the real owners before the house was taken over by the Occupation must have been moderately wealthy at one time. On the gate, of solid oak, was a small white sign with heavy black print, both in English and Japanese, which read: "U.S. Army Property, Unauthorized personnel Keep Out" and "*Tachi-iri kinshi.*"

A maid in kimono and a long-sleeved white apron bowed as she opened the gate.

"*Konnichi-wa. Yoku kimashita,*" she said — so nice of you to have come.

"*Hajime mashite,*" Jo said, returning her bow. Her graying hair, done in a bun, reminded Jo of his mother.

The maid led Jo up a path along side of a garden. Low shrubs, rough stones, a bit of moss and a pond were typically Japanese, though the house itself with mortared walls was Western style, giving a sense of disharmony.

Jo was mildly surprised as he was shown into the living room by the maid, who then disappeared into a back room. Though it was a Sunday, Neal Kramer wore a suit; his wife Carol a silk dress. Their other two guests — a tall gray-haired man in a seersucker suit, and a younger woman wearing a broad-brimmed white hat and a dress with bright flower designs — were Don and Wilma Sheldon. Don was section chief in the civil government branch of the Occupation and Neal's boss. Wilma, Don's wife, said she wasn't working, "just enjoying life in Japan."

"Such a coincidence...hadn't seen Jo since Madison; then Carol bumps into him in a coffee line at a snack bar in Tokyo," Neal said, introducing Jo. "Carol and he were classmates at the Journalism School at the University of Wisconsin."

"Oh, a Nisei then," Don said. Looking at the lone stripe on Jo's sleeve, he asked, "And what's your assignment here in Tokyo?" He spoke with a Boston accent; lines in his face indicated he frowned a lot.

"I'm at ATIS," Jo said.

"Ah, yes. Are you a translator then?"

"I type and proofread."

"Oh," the man said, and in his eyes Jo could see his loss of interest. A PFC, what else should one expect — the expression on his face seemed to say. Then, turning back to Neal, the man continued, "As I was saying regarding the coming elections, I had to tell Nozaka no matter what..." The man went on talking as if Jo did not exist. After Nozaka, the man mentioned Yoshida, Hatoyama, Asanuma and other Japanese political leaders of the day. Jo recognized the names and knew generally where they stood politically, though he was not up-to-date on the latest issues. He did not manage to read the English language *Nippon Times* that regularly while the *Stars and Stripes* hardly covered Japanese politics.

Interesting, Jo thought, Don sounded as if he dealt directly with all these political leaders, maybe was even their personal friend.

"You speak Japanese, then?" Jo asked.

"Well...no," the man said, "don't know the language."

"But Nozaka, the others you talk to?"

"Oh, we communicate," the man said.

"You see," the man went on, turning back to Neal, "democracy is new to these people. They don't have a grasp of the full concept. We have to teach..."

We? He?

"Take for example, the *Eta*, who..."

But before he finished his sentence, Wilma, his wife, pulled Jo away.

"Pooh," she said. "Don's always talking shop. Then winking at Neal, she said, "Let him talk shop with Neal. Neal has to listen; he works for him. But you, Jo, sit with Carol and me.

I've got lots of things I want to ask you."

"Forgive me," Carol said as the three moved to a rattan couch and chairs. "I told Wilma you know a lot about Japan, or at least I thought you did. Now that I think about it, though we sat together in all those classes at J-school, I don't know if you even speak Japanese."

"Speak some, but at a third grade level," Jo said.

"Even that's something," Wilma said. She wished she could converse even a little bit in the language. She said she was fascinated by things Japanese — the art, the theater, literature, dance, music, even calligraphy, which she obviously couldn't read but in which could sense delicate discipline. She said she and Carol took courses at the Officers' Wives Club;

just finished a wonderful study of Japanese art; covered various masters; couldn't remember the names, though, except for Hokusai and Hiroshige. Who was Jo's favorite?

Jo studied Wilma's face as she talked, noticing the differences between her and Carol. Carol had brown hair, a broad face with freckles, and a heavyset body; Wilma, a small pointed nose with pale, almost translucent skin; a small, sharp chin; blue-green eyes always intent; light red hair showing in curls below the brim of her hat. Wilma reminded him of someone, somewhere, years back though he could not quite recall who.

"Who's your favorite Japanese artist?" Wilma repeated.

"Don't know any too well," Jo said.

"I love Hiroshige," Wilma said. "His water colors, you know, of his times, so... Our instructor said any Japanese would know about Hiroshige."

"Well...," Jo hesitated.

"Jo's probably more interested in their literature," Carol said, filling in the pause in the conversation. "I remember, he had short stories published in the school literary magazine."

"Oh," Wilma said, then asked, "Have you read many of the Japanese authors?"

Jo said he had just finished reading a translation of a short story by a new young writer, Mishima.

"You don't read him in his original?" Wilma asked, disappointed. She still reminded him of someone, somewhere.

"No," Jo said. He knew that even the simplest Japanese terms often lost their nuances in translation. But he'd be able to read the originals only with the heavy use of a Japanese-to-English dictionary if they had not been translated. Besides, Mishima, like other Japanese writers, contended that only the Japanese could understand the Japanese; that you had to be one to understand one, a category Jo did not quite fit. He read other translations — of Tanizaki, Shimazaki, Nagai, Soseki — and said the translations often left him unsatisfied.

While they were talking, Carol, who had gone into the kitchen, returned to the hallway and beckoned to Jo.

"Could you help?" she asked. "Mr. and Mrs. Sato are such willing workers, but sometimes they can't understand my English. This roast — I like beef on the rare side. Mr. Sato, though, seems to feel that if the beef is red on the inside, it's not done."

Mr. Sato, who immediately wiped his hands on his apron and bowed as Jo entered the kitchen, was in his late 50's, gray-haired with a ready smile.

"*Sukoshi nama no* ho - - by rare Carol meant a little bit on the raw side," Jo explained in his simple Japanese. "*Ah, sore de...* " Mr. Sato said, then laughed in relief. Mrs. Kramer was such a nice person to work for, he added, but he had never cooked a roast before coming to work for her. "*Re-ru*," he said she said. He found the word in his English-Japanese dictionary — it meant unusual, infrequent, something like that. However, he couldn't figure out how it applied when cooking meat.

As Mrs. Sato, the maid who had earlier met Jo at the gate and who was cleaning some vegetables near by, moved over to add her thanks, Jo thought of his own parents. Jo did not know what sort of work Mr. Sato may have been doing before, but wondered. They had a certain dignity in their manners, and like his own parents, circumstances resulting from the war may have forced them into domestic work.

"I was going to ask you about Saikaku," Wilma said as Jo and Carol returned. "From what I've read of his translations, I think he's great."

"He's one of my favorites, too," Jo said. "But even the Japanese don't read him in his original any more, he wrote too long ago; his works have to be translated into modern Japanese."

Must be like the ballads at the *Kabuki*, those sung by the *shamisen* players, Wilma said, or at least that was what she was told.

Kabuki — and suddenly Jo recalled who Wilma reminded him of: Mrs. Davies — the same color hair, the unusually pale skin — his fifth grade teacher at Jefferson Union Elementary School. League of Nations Day... each student was to bring in a phonograph record of music of the country their parents or grandparents came from. In a last minute rush, Jo borrowed a record from his father's music album, not even sure of what it was.

In class, Mrs. Davies praised the lively dance music Nino Gomez brought; she thought the German polka a lot of fun; the Slovenian songs haunting. When she put Jo's record on (he could remember Mrs. Davies bending over to wind the crank on the phonograph player), there was a complete silence as the off-key guttural sounds came from the machine. After a minute or two, a student here, another there, began to titter, then laugh; soon it seemed the whole class was laughing.

Mrs. Davies turned the record off before it was half over. The red of her face almost matched that of her hair as she rapped on the desk with a ruler. But when the class was quieted, she couldn't find anything to say. The music was as strange to her as it was to the students. Jo learned only later that his father's album was a collection of ballads from the old *Kabuki* theater.

"You've had such an advantage, a chance to know the culture of two worlds," Wilma said.

Jo just shrugged.

The dinner was fine. Everything on the table came from the Army commissary — the roast, sent frozen, originally from Chicago; the lettuce, radishes, cucumbers and celery grown hydroponically by the commissary; the potatoes, onions and carrots, sent by ship from California.

"The vegetables I see in the stands along the streets, are they the same as ours back home?" Wilma asked. "The carrots and cucumbers, for instance. They must be a foot or more long."

"They're the same," Jo said.

"Ah, but you mustn't eat them," Don, her husband broke in. his frown fit the lines of his forehead. "Dysentery, worms — you don't know what you might get. They use night soil."

"You can sterilize them," Jo said. "For salads, just run some boiling water over them."

"Still...," Don said. He recited Occupation rules — don't eat in any but those designated "Class A" restaurants, don't stay in any but Army-authorized hotels, don't drink at untested

water fountains, don't buy any food from street vendors, don't..."

"Don't...don't...don't. Seems the only word the Army knows," Wilma broke in. "How am I ever going to get to know Japan, meet some genuine Japanese?"

As she finished, she caught Jo's eyes. "Wasn't implying anything about you," she said. It's just that..."

"No problems," Jo said. He looked at Neal and Carol, Don and Wilma — aliens in another people's land; they so much more than he. Genuine Japanese — he had a whole list of relatives and family friends his mother and father had given him, many of whom he had visited. He wasn't sure of what Wilma was looking for.

"Have you ever tried eating the food of vendors with their mobile stands along the streets near the rail stations?" Wilma asked. "I've always been tempted to peek behind their curtains, see what they have."

"They've got about everything," Jo said. "*Onden, yakitori, tempura, sushi,* hot rice dishes, noodles, what have you."

"Sounds wonderful," Wilma said. "Don, though, won't have anything to do with them."

"You know the rules," Don said.

"Yes," Wilma said, "don't...don't...don't."

"You've been on the Army tours," her husband said. "You've been to Nikko, Karuizawa, Hakone; the theaters, the temples. We've gone to Kyoto twice."

"Still," she said, "the only people we seem to really meet are others with the Occupation or those catering to us. I envy Jo. He's got such a wonderful opportunity."

It was dark and things looked more familiar as Jo made his way back to the Shimbashi station. The street peddlers were back; more than half of the stools at the bar in the *Basha* were occupied; the smell of cooking spiced the air; the plaster of paris mermaid almost looked becoming again in her flood of colored lights.

Jo glanced at his watch; seemed too early to return to his billets. Down the street he could see a new Tokyo-style coffee house. The building, painted a garish reddish-purple with a neon peacock of purple, blue and red, on its roof, hovered over the rest of the buildings on the block. Curious, he decided to go in.

"*Komban-wa,*" a young girl in a short-skirted, light blue uniform with gold braid greeted him. "*O hitori desuka* — are you alone?"

Jo nodded. She looked like a majorette in a high school band.

The girl led Jo into a large, ballroom-like hall. Tables and chairs crowded the main floor. Small booths lined the sides, and as Jo looked up, he could see tiers of booths reaching almost to the ceiling three stories above. From the center of the ceiling, a mirrored, multi-faceted ball reflected red, yellow, purple and blue colored spotlights as it rotated slowly on its axis.

Jo asked for a side booth away from the flickering lights and settled back to wait for his coffee.

He recognized the song in the background music — a Japanese song about a white flower, a flower of love. Though the hall was smoky and crowded, upholstery covered the walls to muffle the sound. As the waitress brought his coffee he noticed two girls being escorted to the booth behind him, one wearing a pill-box type hat like that worn by the young woman who, earlier during the day, ran when he tried to ask her for directions to get to the Kramers.

Later, after the two had given their orders, Jo heard one of the young women say, "*Anone, kiyo hidoi* — a really frightening thing happened to me today."

"*Honto-ni*" — really — she kept repeating to add emphasis. "An Occupation soldier, looked like a Nisei, tried to approach me," she said. "Didn't know what he wanted, but she ran. He couldn't have been up to any good. It was horrible."

"*So ne*," her companion agreed. The Nisei...bad types. Loose women, *sake*, the black market — seems that's all they're interested in. She said she had never met one, hoped she never would.

Balls, Jo reacted. He was tempted to stick his head around the partition and tell the girls that all he had wanted were simple directions. But he did nothing, feeling that rather than changing their minds, he might just upset them further.

Later, on his way back to the station, the conversation he overheard between the two girls lingered in his mind. Growing up in California, he was conscious from early school days of the anti-Asian, especially anti-Japanese, prejudice. U.S. laws prevented his parents from becoming U.S. citizens; California law said only U.S. citizens could own land in the state, thus barring them from ever owning the land they farmed; Asians could not buy homes in certain areas; interracial marriages often were not recognized; unwritten social barriers were widespread.

But in Japan? Naively, he had thought being of Japanese descent he'd be accepted as one of their own. Obviously, the two girls at the coffee house did not. With relatives and family friends he sensed no alienation. But others? He half-smiled at the irony of it all. In America he faced prejudice because he was of Japanese descent. Was he being prejudged in Japan because he, though of the same blood, was an American?

On his way to the station, he passed in front of the "Oasis" again; saw the make-believe mermaid in its colorful flood of neon lights. Somehow, even with the darkness shrouding its reality, it no longer seemed becoming. His life in Japan, was it as superficial?

But as he looked, he made up his mind. He'd get out of the Army, go back to school, learn more about Japan, then return to Tokyo, live and work there, be a Japanese for a while whether they wanted him or not.

Chapter Twelve
Stupid *Haole*, Stupid Gook

"They (the Japanese) failed to accept the thesis that a Communist victory in Korea would be a portentous threat to their own freedom and security...Therefore, the United States devoted much time and effort toward a successful conclusion of Japanese peace treaty." (Borton, Japan's Modern Century, page 435)

Sept. 8, 1951: Japanese-American Peace and Security Treaties signed in San Francisco. (ibid, page 442)

○

Jo fixed his eyes on those of the Major as the man shouted at him. The face was flush; the gray eyes angry.

"Damn you, soldier; you're on guard duty. Where was your salute? You're not here to talk to old woman on the sidewalk."

The Major was thin, not very tall, only two or three inches taller than Jo. Jo continued to look directly at the man. The son of bitch. The man's nose — its pale skin almost translucent — quivered. Whatever was bugging the guy's ass? But Jo was not about to blink. He had been trying to help the old woman. The Major could shove it.

"Well?" the Major said.

"Yes, Sir," Jo said, and saluted.

The Major returned the salute, then turned on his heels and walked to his jeep. His driver, in the blue and gray uniform of Japanese civilians hired by the Occupation, gave a sharp salute, which the Major snappily returned.

The old woman, who had been the cause of the scene and had watched it all, moved meekly toward Jo as the jeep left. She bowed, her weather-worn face expressing concern, and said, "*Gomen nasai,*" then quickly scurried off.

"*Shimpai-nai,*" Jo said, but she was out of earshot. Hell, he didn't even get a chance to finish answering her question.

Jo had been standing at his guard post at the main entrance to the NYK Building, headquarters of the Allied Translators and Interpreters Service in downtown Tokyo, watching the people going by — groups of students in black uniforms, couples strolling, an occasional family group. They were either going to or coming from the nearby outer gate to the Imperial

Palace grounds. The occasional fleeting glance betrayed their curiosity at seeing a Japanese face in an American uniform. Only the small children with family groups were open, some even pointing while being restrained by their mothers.

When Jo first saw the old woman, he could see immediately that she was lost. She had walked in from the corner about five yards, then walked back to read the street sign, then back again. Her baggy workpants — *"mompei"* — were clean but faded; her canvas shoes worn; her blouse a dull blue with polka dots. A piece of cotton cloth was tied bonnet fashion over her head. She carried a reed mat under her left arm; a brown, paper-wrapped bundle in her right hand. Maybe a farm woman in a strange part of the city on her way home after having sold her produce.

As she shuffled up to Jo, she bowed and asked the direction to Tokyo Station.

"Sochira. Ni buraku gurai," Jo said, pointing in the direction of the station, which, though only two blocks away, could not be seen because of the trees and tall buildings.

"Eh?" the woman responded, not having understood his Japanese. So Jo moved down the three steps at his post at the entrance to the building to the sidewalk to explain. He was about to tell her she would have to turn right to the side entrance used by the Japanese — the main gates were reserved for Occupation personnel — when the Major appeared.

"That damn chicken shit," Jo said as he stepped back up the steps to his post.

After getting off from guard duty the next morning, Jo went up to the mess hall on the eighth floor. His unit was billeted, ate and worked in the same NYK Building. He'd eat and take a quick shower before going to the publications section where he proofread prisoner-of-war interrogation reports from the fighting in Korea and did occasional typing.

A group of GI's stood in front of him in the chow line. He didn't know them and wasn't paying much attention when one of the GI's, half mumbling, ended his sentence with "...those stupid gooks."

Jo looked up; caught the man's eyes. The man, brown-haired and blue-eyed, seemed a bit embarrassed, turned his head slightly, then continued talking but in a much lower voice. Stupid gooks — stupid *haoles* was Jo's silent reply.

Jo arrived in his office still smarting over his run-in with the Major. Even before he sat down, he saw Sergeant Garr, the first sergeant in charge of the GI's in the section, approach.

"Hey, Jo," he said, "why don't you go up stairs and put on a clean shirt?"

"Why?" Jo asked.

"You're going before the NCO board."

"Me? What for?"

"I put you in for a promotion, dummy," Garr smiled. "We want to make better use of you."

"Oh, Christ...," Jo said, then stopped. He didn't ask for a promotion; didn't want one. Garr, an Army career man, would not be able to believe that. He had good intentions, though, and Jo said "Okay," then left to put on a fresh shirt. He'd go along with the show.

Jo stiffened the moment he walked into the room where the NCO board met. There sat the thin major — like a judge in court — flanked by two captains, behind a heavy oak desk. The American flag stood to his right, the dark blue colors of the 302nd Military Intelligence Co. on the left. Both flags stood in highly polished brass stands and were trimmed with gold braid.

Jo looked the Major in the face as he saluted. The Major showed no recognition — maybe he wanted to be objective, not remember the GI he had bawled out the evening before; but more likely he could not recognize one Oriental GI from another.

"How long do you intend to stay in the Army?" the Major asked as he opened the questioning. Jo read the man's nameplate over a row of campaign ribbons on his chest — "Kellog." The two captains pretended to show interest in what was expected to be routine. Give the right answers and he'd get the promotion.

"I'm getting out as soon as I can, Sir," Jo replied.

Silence.

"You getting married, Corporal?" the Major asked.

"No, Sir."

The Major frowned. The two captains now showed some real interest.

"Why'd you join the Army?" the Major then asked.

"I was about to be drafted, Sir."

More silence.

"Why are you before us anyway?"

"I didn't ask to be, Sir," Jo said. Neither was he there to kiss any asses.

"I don't like your attitude, Soldier," the Major said. The two captains along side nodded in agreement. Then the Major, cocking his head like a teacher talking to an erring student, said "Nisei soldiers — a lot of them in this very unit — have a brilliant history with the U.S. Army. Why can't you..."

"Sorry, Sir," Jo said. He was a soldier, not a Nisei soldier.

"Dismissed," the Major said.

"Yes, Sir," Jo said. Stupid *haole* — stupid gook.

By evening Jo had forgotten about the Major and the Major's displeasure. Jo sat in the lobby of the Old Kaijo Hotel, which housed American civilian female personnel, mainly stenographers and other clerical workers, waiting for Lani. He hoped she might have some word on whether he could get out of the typing and proofreading job he was stuck with.

It was 6:30 p.m.; he had waited 20 minutes and was about to go when she came through the front door. Long, wavy, jet black hair; brown eyes, brown skin, a flat Polynesian nose, Lani Oshiro; said she was half Japanese, a quarter Portuguese and an eighth each Hawaiian and *haole*.

"Got some good news for you," she said as she sat beside him. "He likes your stuff."

"Who? The Budahead, Lt. Tanaka?"

"No," she said. "The Major, Tanaka's boss. Tanaka was in charge when you took the test because the Major was off. Major said your stuff is pretty good; that you at least know some-thing about China. He said the psy-war section needs writers who at least know about Mao, Chou, Liu Shao-chi, the 'Long March,' Yenan, that sort of stuff."

"Did some reading on China," Jo said.

"Major was wondering: your files show you worked on a newspaper, how come they have you proofreading and typing."

"Hell, this is the Army."

"Anyway, the Major said it was a big waste; that we could use you."

"Swell," Jo said. "What happens next?"

She explained. A reorganization was underway. Psy-War was being shifted from G-2 to G-3. While Wsy-war was part of G-2, no transfer was needed, only a simple memo from the Major to Jo's boss would have gotten Jo into the Psy-War writing unit. With the reorganization, however, Jo would have to initiate the move himself, put in for a transfer.

"It ought to be a simple thing," she said. Then, pulling a brown envelope from her briefcase, she said, "You know, the copy of your file you gave me. I filled out the forms you need. Here, all you have to do is sign them."

"Thanks," Jo said. He'd look the papers over later. "But how'd you know about the forms?"

"Didn't I tell you? Major's on the NCO board as well. You know, where they control transfers and pro..."

"NCO board?" Jo interrupted. "What's the Major's name?"

"Kellog. Major Rolland Kellog. Thought everyone knew who he was."

"Guess I know him, in a way," Jo said.

"I know some GI's don't like him," she said. "But I think he's okay. You'll like him."

"Yeah, I bet," Jo said.

"You crazy, man?" Tets asked.

"What do you mean?" Jo replied, surprised.

"This shit about Korea. Somebody said you're volunteering to go over."

"Bull. Who said that?"

"That *wahine*, the one in the Psy-War section. What's her name, Lani."

"She tell you?"

"No. But another *wahine* in the same office, the one from Maui, said Lani was typing out some transfer papers for you."

"Oh, that. That's nothing," Jo said. "I've been trying to get into the writing unit at Psy-War, that's all. She typed out the forms for me, but I haven't signed anything."

"Be careful, man," Tets said. "You know the rule — ask for a transfer and they ship you to Korea. They'll ship us over pretty soon anyway. Why you want to push things?"

"Yeah, but..."

"No 'buts.' Hey, we go drink. Forget the Army. Relax. Be happy. You don't like being in Japan or something?"

"Shit. You know that's not it."

With that, Jo, who was on his bunk in his underwear, got up, picked up his towel and put on his *zori* to head for the showers. Tets, already dressed in his khakis, grabbed his hat and headed for the door.

"Sei and I, we're going to the usual place in Shimbashi," Tets said. "Join us there. We'll drink some beer; get those crazy ideas out of your head."

Jo felt the warm water from the shower run down his body and watched the soap suds disappear in streamlets with each twist of his torso. Crazy ideas, maybe. But being in Japan? Of course, he liked it. He had arrived in the country a year earlier aboard the troopship, the "General Pope." At the Army docks in Oakland, the troops were already on board when they heard the news of the war in Korea. After a few days out to sea the ship's mimeographed news sheet reported President Truman's decision to send U.S. ground troops as well as air support. That meant most of the 1,600 or so GI's on board would be sent straight to Korea. Some seemed excited by the prospect; others were scared. Jo was neither, though he wondered how he would react if he got into actual combat.

Jo was lucky. Soldiers at GHQ in Tokyo were among the first to be sent to the war in Korea. So when the Pope arrived in Japan, the 16 soldiers on board originally assigned to GHQ were sent there to fill the gap thus created.

The night the Pope pulled into Yokohama Harbor, Jo could not sleep — not because of Korea but because he would be seeing Japan. He was on the upper deck the next morning long before chow time for a look at the shore. All he could see through the fog was an island; its grass, bushes and trees, all a lush green, giving off steamy vapor even in the cool of the morning. As the ship gently rose and settled with the swells, he looked for houses, signs of people, but could see no one. He was in Japan; he wanted to see some Japanese.

Later, on a truck rumbling along the streets of downtown Tokyo toward the Finance building where incoming GI's were temporarily billeted, he was struck by the bustle and energy of the Japanese, even laborers — men and women — putting broken bricks into piles, sweeping and clearing debris. He could see buses and occasional large trucks compete with street cars, three-wheeled pickups, battered charcoal-burning taxis, and bicycles for the limited space on the streets.

He was stirred then by what he saw; remembered an urge to be one of them, an urge he still sometimes felt. At the same time he was glad he was a GI. He could not quite put his fingers on why, but deep down he strongly resented the patronizing and smugness he sensed among Occupation personnel in their dealings with the Japanese. The condescension he saw on the Major's face as the Major saluted the jeep driver was the same look Jo saw on the faces of the others: officers, both *haole* and Nisei; Department of Army civilians in the publications section where he worked, both supervisors and clerks; on the face of the GI who spoke of "stupid gooks."

Asses, let them lord it over the Japanese, not him.

When Jo walked out of the NYK Building and headed for Tokyo Station, it was about 8:30 p.m. but still light out. It had cooled some, and after his shower, his summer khakis felt comfortable. Also, while showering, he had half sorted out his plans. He'd forget trying to get into the Psy-War unit. It could have been good experience, but the Major... He doubted if the Major would have wanted him anyway. Meanwhile, he would continue to play soldier at ATIS — getting his boots polished and standing guard duty when he had to; working with the fat-assed Army wives and other civilians, many of them ex-GI's who couldn't find civilian jobs elsewhere; putting up with the goddam brass. He wasn't about to sign the transfer papers, not about to volunteer for Korea. Tets was right; why push things.

Jo was still thinking to himself as he approached the entrance to the red brick station but noticed a group of GI's trying to hail a cab. Their skins were pale; their uniforms didn't quite seem to fit — could've just come out of a hospital. One GI — blond, small — seemed with the group though he stood a little bit aside.

As Jo walked by, the GI looked up, there was instant recognition, for Jo, also a shock.

"Fancy meeting you here," the GI said. He seemed genuinely glad though his voice lacked resonance.

Jo remembered the face — the tiny pointed nose, the pale blue eyes, the thin delicate cheek bones. It was the same kid all right, the one at the replacement depot at Camp Stoneman, then on the troopship. But he was far too pale. The innocent curiosity, formerly the most noticeable thing about his eyes, was gone.

"Hey, you remember me, don't you?" the GI asked.

"God, of course. It was just the surprise," Jo said. He couldn't recall the kid's name, but could remember him well. The kid was 17 going on 18 when they were at Camp Stoneman. A high school dropout; joined the Army because he had nothing else to do; his mother kept getting on his back.

"Buddy of mine, used to be stationed here before they shipped him to Korea. He's supposed to meet me here, show me some of his former hangouts," the kid said. "How about you? Haven't seen you since we got off the Pope in Yokohama. You stationed here?"

"Yeah," Jo said. "Been stationed here all the time, just up the street."

"Lucky you," the kid said. He swallowed a bit; looked like he might throw up as his face turned red. A moment later, though, his face turned back to normal. "Sorry," he said, "it's the first time they let us out of the hospital. Sometimes I still get a bit woozy. They said I'll be all right in a couple of weeks, though."

"Certainly hope so," Jo said. "Which unit were you with?"

"Seventh Cav," the kid said. "They put us on a train to Sasebo the same day we got off the Pope in Yokohama. They shipped us right over to Pusan."

"Must've been bad," Jo said. This was the kid who thought Jo was smart because Jo worked crossword puzzles; the kid who kept coming to Jo with questions. "You think they'll ship us over?" the kid must have asked a dozen times before the official announcement was made.

As Jo looked into his face, the kid sensed the question in Jo's mind.

"Got it in the gut this time," he said. "Was in the leg the first time."

His voice indicated no emotion. As he shifted his feet and turned to watch a passing car, he look tired, not old, but drained of feeling. For a moment he gazed off at nothing, then looked back at Jo.

"You know," he said. "I don't care anymore. In another couple of weeks I'll be well again. They're going to ship me back to Korea, back to the Seventh Cav. I don't want to go. I'll go because they'll make me. But I don't care anymore."

The lights of the city were just starting to come on as the local electric train pulled out of Tokyo Station — Yuraku-cho next, then Shimbashi, where he'd get off. In the distance he could see the red neon sign of the YMCA; the red, blue and green lights of the Daito Hotel, the name written in both *Romaji* and *Kanji*; the Dentsu Building, on whose roof blinking yellow and white lights formed a replica of the world globe. Along the narrow, unpaved street next to the tracks, red paper lanterns were beginning to stand out in the growing darkness. A *sake* shop here, a noodle stand there, a *pachinko* parlor further down, stood amid shuttered houses, their wooden rain doors closed tightly for the night. Jo had seen the sight countless times. His eyes now, however, searched out the details — he wanted to fix the scene in his memory. He would not be seeing it many more times.

Come Monday, he would sign the transfer papers Lani had typed for him, take it to the CO's office himself, give it to the company sergeant and not tell anyone else. When his orders came he would simply tell Tets, Sei, Lani and the others that his number just came up. He was only putting in for a transfer; he could honestly say that he had not volunteered for Korea.

"I don't care anymore," the kid had repeated. He didn't have to say it; Jo could see it in the kid's face, his eyes.

The Author, taking a break on the granite bridge of the dry pond at the Kim Koo House in Soul (October, 1951).

Chapter XIII
The Pond

July 21, 1951: Armistice negotiations to end the Korean War begin in Kaesong. June 13, 1952: U.S. Air Force bombs Yalu River power installations to induce a more cooperative attitude in the truce talks. (Max Hasting, "The Korean War," Simon and Schuster, 1987, page 349)

"Many United Nations veterans came home from Korea to discover that their experience was of no interest whatsoever to their fellow countrymen. The war seemed an unsatisfactory, inglorious, and thus unwelcome memory." (ibid, page 330)

O

"Hey Lee, what're you guys doing?" Jo asked. He could see through the bushes in the garden to where Lee, a corporal, stood with Kim Senior and two other Korean workmen attached to the unit.

Then, before they could answer, Jo saw to his horror what they were about.

"Christ, what're you doing to the pond?" Jo asked.

"Shit, you can see for yourself," Lee said. "We're lining it with cement. It's the goddam Captain's orders."

"But...," Jo started to say, then seeing the look on Lee's face, said, "Hell, I know it's not your fault."

"Fish," Lee fumed. "Fish. All the *pilau* bugger wants is fish in the pond. I tell the bugger the pond's not meant to hold water; that the cement would wreck the looks of the whole garden. But the *haole* bugger, he can't understand. Fish. Somebody ought to stuff a few up his ass."

Gray blotches of cement and empty sacks were scattered on the pathway; a pile of sand and another of gravel half buried some of the green shrubbery; a battered wooden trough bent the small bush it was crowded against. The sacks, sand and gravel could be removed, the area tidied; but the pond itself already was lined half way up with soggy, wet cement. Once dried, heavy picks or a jackhammer would be needed to remove the cement.

That damn Captain. The garden was something special for all the GIs of the unit. For Lee, of Korean ancestry from Hawaii, it seemed to mean a lot more. Lee was the one who originally introduced Jo to the garden and the pond when Jo first joined the unit the previous summer.

When Jo had first joined the unit, he had come by troop train from Taegu. Lee was at the train station in Seoul with a jeep to pick Jo up. As they drove away from the station, all Jo could see was devastation. The freight yard next to the station was a mass of twisted rails, punctured and rusting tank cars, loose wheels, skeletons of box cars, a burned out locomotive, and mounds of pipes and rubble. The scene on the way to the compound was dominated by piles of bricks, partial walls of buildings with no roofs and glassless windows, corrugated galvanized metal sheets covering hovels, sidewalks which disappeared under debris, and caves in the hillsides with straw mats at their entrances showing that was where people lived.

Along the streets, groups of children dressed in rags but smiling, sometimes waved and shouted, "Hi Joe." But the grown-ups — women in baggy denim work pants and half-graying blouses, an occasional old man with a stove-pipe hat and white clothing, and ROK soldiers, many with steel helmets, rifles and backpacks — ignored the jeep.

Going through the gate into the unit's compound was like entering a park area. The compound covered about half an acre and was encircled by a high brick wall. The main building — two-storied with a pillared front — stood in the center. Small shell holes pockmarked its facade, but the building was not extensively damaged. The garden was discreetly off to the right and hardly noticeable from the front of the house.

"Hey, you've got to see something before you see anything else," Lee had said even before the jeep came to a full stop. "The houseboys will take care of your gear. Follow me."

The pond and its garden came into full view as Lee led Jo along a pebbled pathway through some bushes. A mound of smooth stones, partially covered with small flowering plants and low gray shrubbery, formed a backdrop for the circular pond. The side of the pond was lined with similar stones; its bottom was covered with yellow sand. Two small dry streamlets led from the pond in and around the garden, while seven or eight huge slabs of roughly hewn granite formed a natural bridge over part of the pond and the streamlets. The pebbled pathway led in and around the entire garden. The only sign of the war was a pile of sandbags — already rotting and losing their contents — in the far corner next to one of the compound's front gate.

The pond and the garden from then on seemed the only remaining bit of sanity and beauty in war-torn Seoul. On a spring day, a person could stretch out full on one of the granite slabs and soak up the warmth of the sun; in the winter the snow partially covered the stones and the shrubbery, enhancing their message of nature. Cementing the pond — like dropping an off-color blob on a silk print — destroyed the harmony of the garden.

"Pilau" — stinker — the Hawaiian word Lee used fit the Captain completely.

Leaving Lee still upset, Jo returned to his battered desk, scrounged from a bombed-out school building, to finish editing a half-dozen prisoner-of-war interrogation reports. His eyes quickly skimmed the reports for unit identifications, locations of capture, then ranks — an artillery captain, 272nd Regiment, and two corporals from the neighboring 273rd, both of the 40th Division of the Chinese People's "Volunteer" 60th Army. Nothing new, nothing headquarters would get excited about.

As Jo almost mechanically crossed out verbiage and did some minor rewriting, his mind still focussed on the Captain. When the Captain first came to the unit — a new C.O. came almost every three or four months — Jo briefed him on what was needed by the order-of-battle section at headquarters. The section's main concerns were to learn of any new units and/or changes in deployment on the communist side.

Jo made mention of the so-called "monkey brigade" — several Chinese PWs with straight faces had reported that such a brigade existed with the monkeys trained to fire machine guns and throw grenades, that only the squad leaders were human — to see how the Captain would respond. The man half-smiled, but made no comment. He did not say much about anything else either, leaving Jo and the others to wonder what sort of man he was.

A few days later, Jo was at his desk when he heard the Captain talking to Kim Senior.

"No buts," Jo heard the Captain say. "Paint the U.N. symbol on that wood. Now, that's an order."

The Captain then entered the room off of the foyer where Jo sat and said, "Good morning Sergeant. I've just told Kim I want the U.N. symbol on that piece of wood at the foot of the stairs. You see that he does a good job of it."

"Sir, you mean that hardwood panel?"

"Exactly."

"But it'll be ruined, Sir. It's..."

"It's just a piece of wood," the Captain insisted. "I want it painted. It's an order. We're the Eighth Army interrogation team. We got to get some class into this outfit."

"Yes Sir," Jo said; but as he looked at the Captain — tall, lean, his light brown hair cropped in a crew cut — he wondered, is the man serious? Or is he trying to play some role he had seen in a wartime movie?

The panel the Captain wanted painted was a solid piece of maple about the height of a man's shoulders, embedded in a log. Its surface was polished smooth, probably by daily wiping over the years by maids using rice bran, which gave the wood a transparent finish that brought out the gracefulness of the gnarled rings of its grain.

The panel was a center piece of the house. The house previously had been the home and office of Kim Koo, one of Korea's top liberal politicians, who was shot in an upstairs bedroom just before the outbreak of the Korean War, and may have reflected the man's tastes. The downstairs office rooms were Western in style and feeling despite a dragon's head carved into the molding above the doors and a peacock design in the stained glass window overlooking the porch in the rear.

Upstairs, off of the main hallway, *tatami* covered the floors; the master bedroom had a moon-shaped entrance; shoji separated the rooms, and intricate floral patterns were carved into the natural redwood just below the ceiling. The rooms and hallways had lacquered dressers and chairs of orange and green on shiny black, screens with misty mountain scenes, and bamboo-trimmed tiny tables.

The panel, located at the foot of the stairs, prepared a person for the change in decor between the two floors.

Kim Senior did a good job of painting the pale blue U.N. symbol on the panel. The curves in the design were smooth; the color uniform.

"I finish," Kim said as he approached Jo. "Come see."

"That's fine," Jo said as he looked at the shiny coat of wet paint. "The Captain should be happy."

It could have been the inflection in Jo's voice, but Kim seemed to sense Jo's feeling. Looking Jo in the eye, Kim, whose bearded and wrinkled face showed a wry smile, said, "The

Captain..." and then made circular motions with his index finger around his right ear.

"*Shoga-nai yatsu,*" Jo said in Japanese since he could not think of any Korean words to describe the Captain as crude and tasteless, and wasn't sure if Kim would have understood if English were used.

"*So-ne,*" Kim nodded, "like donkey;" then burst out laughing.

Other changes took place after the Captain's arrival. Being removed from the main Eighth Army headquarters compound, no one in interrogation unit paid much attention to the spit and polish of soldiering. Most of the enlisted men were of Asian ancestry and because they never bothered to wear their stripes, a standing joke among visitors to the unit was that they, at times, could not tell the GIs from the houseboys. But no one cared; the work was done.

With the new C.O., however, the orders went around — polish your boots, sew on your stripes, press your fatigues. Crap, some said, but it was all part of being in the Army so there was little grumbling. Besides, it gave the houseboys and the Korean women who did the laundry a bit of extra work and pay.

Loper's case, however, was different. Loper, the unit's mechanic, was drafted off of a Nevada ranch, knew all about fixing jeeps, trucks, tractors or anything with gasoline motors long before the Army got him. He was quiet and conscientious, kept the unit's jeeps and trucks well-tuned and in good running order. Good-natured, he got along with everyone in the unit as well as the houseboys, the "mama-sans," the ROK officers and other Koreans he had to deal with.

Not too long after the C.O. had arrived, Jo, for the first time, heard Loper gripe.

"It's crazy," Loper said. "The Captain sees some brass at headquarters with an air-conditioned jeep and thinks he ought to have one too. The jeep has to be closed up; the whole back seat taken out. Outside of Seoul it's still a combat zone; we couldn't go anywhere else with the dumb jeep. I'm not going to do it."

"You know what'll happen if you don't," someone said.

"Sure. He'll transfer my ass. But I'm still not going to do it."

Several days later a new mechanic arrived, unannounced. A week later Loper was transferred to the 7th Cav along the front even though he had only a month or so before his scheduled discharge.

The unit Jo was in was small — six officers and only a dozen or so enlisted men at headquarters and equal numbers of officers and men with field teams in Yongdungpo, Chunchon and Sokcho-ri. Even with the arrival of the new CO, the relationship between the enlisted men and the officers remained informal. In the evenings after work, the officers sat in one side of the basement room, which became the recreation room when it wasn't being used as the mess hall, the enlisted men on the other. Occasionally an officer would join the GIs for a beer, or if there was a poker or crap game going, the GIs and officers were mixed. The Captain showed up in the evenings occasionally, but after Loper's transfer, his appearance in the evenings became rare. The GIs could sense the coolness between the Captain and the other officers.

The Captain was not all bad. He got a new mimeograph machine for the unit, new stoves for the field units, and long overdue rest and recuperation leaves for several of the GIs. (Most had what the Army said were essential language skills and for a long time were not allowed to take any "R & R's.") His insistence on neatness also, though few would admit to it, made life more pleasant. Jo, like several of the others, began to feel that maybe the Captain wasn't any worse than most of the other COs who had run the unit.

Things seem to be settling down when the pond became an issue.

"Hey, Ho-san, get one of those papers for me," Jo asked one of the Korean houseboys when he heard the jingle of bells of a Korean news vender running by on the street with his one-page "Extra." It wasn't about the war or a political change as Jo had originally thought. Instead, the news sheet said water was to be turned on in the mains of that section of the city where the compound was located. For the first time since the bombings early in the war, water would run out of the faucets in the area, though only for a few hours each day.

It was big news for the Koreans in the neighborhood. They would no longer have to lug water in jugs and cans from a well often a hundred yards or more to their homes for everything from drinking to cooking to washing. The GIs were told the water was not potable. But someone thought of setting up a shower in the building, a luxury — even if the water was always cold — after having used metal helmets as buckets to wash out of for so long.

The Captain thought it would be a good idea to fill up the pond and put in some live fish.

A few nights later, as Jo was going down to the recreation room for some beer, he could hear Kuzik's voice rising in agitation even before he was halfway down.

"What do you think of a man like that?" Kuzik was asking Lee. Kuzik — tall, slim with sharply pointed features — was leaning over Lee as he talked. "Here, tell Sarge what happened today," Kuzik said when he saw Jo.

"It's the pond," Lee said. "We've been trying to fill it for the past three days when the water in the taps was running. But the pond doesn't hold water. Told the Captain. It fills up, then by evening the water is gone. The Captain insists, though, that we keep trying. Today I am out in front when I see this Korean talking to the guard at the gate. So I go over to find out what he wants. Man said he represents the families who live on the hill above us. When we keep the taps on down here, no water goes up to the houses above us. He asked that I take him to the Captain so he could ask that we turn off the taps occasionally."

"So?"

"So I take him into the building and have him wait outside the door while I go in to see the Captain."

"And you know Sarge," Kuzik butted in, "you know what the Captain told Lee to tell the man — I was in the mail room so I could hear every word. 'Tell the man to go fuck himself. We don't have to listen to any of these bastards,' the Captain says. Imagine."

"It's what the man said," Lee nodded. "Didn't really know what to tell the Korean. Hope he doesn't speak much English. He could hear every word. I told the man in Korean that the Captain was busy, that I'd take the matter up with him when he wasn't so rushed."

A few days later, word came down from the central front that maybe the long awaited Chinese summer offensive was starting; if not, at least there seemed to be a lot of enemy redeployment. Three soldiers of a Chinese reconnaissance squad were captured. Head-quarters started yelling for more information: were there any prisoners from a new unit? Were they with a defensive or an offensive group? Did we take any more PWs? Any CIC reports from the sector?

Several days later it was learned that the redeployment involved a change in positions by two of the North Korean divisions which moved from the west coast of the Korean Peninsula to the east coast, with the Chinese taking up the positions on the front that the North Koreans had left. No offensive developed, but Jo was busy and did not have time to give the pond much thought. He also had half-forgotten that the one-year extension on his enlistment was about up. By the time the work slowed, his orders for shipment home had already arrived.

On the day of his departure, Jo went into the garden to give it one last look. Lee and Kuzik, who were to drive him to the railway station, were with him along with Kim Senior. As Jo had feared, the drying cement had turned to an ugly, off-color white.

"Suppose I'll have to turn on the tap again pretty soon, try to fill it up," Lee said.

"Hope it still leaks," Kuzik said.

"Shit, let's go," Jo said after saying goodbye to Kim Senior. Jo wanted to remember the garden as it was.

○

Jo felt uncomfortable as he walked in the hot California sun. Small maple trees along the sidewalk offered some shade, but hardly enough. He saw no one else in uniform and felt badly out of place.

Seeing a cafe with a neon sign saying "air-conditioned," he walked in. It was his first time out of camp since leaving the troopship. As he made his way to the bar, he sensed the strangeness of an atmosphere he had forgotten.

"Hey Sarge," a voice rang out. This was Berkeley, California, who the hell would know him here? He turned toward the voice, but because of a glare from the window, could not make out who it was.

"Over here," the voice said. "Come join us."

The voice was familiar but something was missing.

"Don't tell me you've already forgotten?" came the voice again; then came recognition.

"Captain," Jo said, hesitated, then decided to join him. "Couldn't see who it was at first, then when I could I almost didn't recognize you in civilian clothes."

"It's not Captain anymore," the man said. "It's just Hobart Horner. Call me Hobe."

"Sure," Jo said, though he felt it would take some time before he'd get around to calling the man Hobe.

"They flew me home a couple of weeks after you had left. Saved all that time it would have taken me by troopship. I got my discharge today. But here, let me introduce you," the Captain said, turning to a man seated opposite him.

"This is Jim Slater. He teaches at the University here. History. Jim, this is Sarge; used to be with my unit in Seoul. Could never get the pronunciation of his Japanese name."

"Jim here used to be my roommate at school," the Captain said when Jo was seated. "We're both from Santa Cruz. Gave him a call while I wait for my wife to drive up to get me. But what are you doing in Berkeley? You from this area, too?"

"Naw, not any more," Jo said. "Remember Dr. Soo at the Red Cross Hospital in Seoul? Promised him I would look up his daughter if I had the chance. She's going to school here. Went to the address the doctor gave me, but the landlady said she was out, to come back later. So I'm killing time."

"I remember the hospital. But what about you?" the Captain asked. "Any plans?"

"Don't know yet," Jo said. "Been in the Army almost four years now. Seems like ages. Want to get back to New York first, see my parents and others. Might go to school, take some courses on the Far East. Much more interested in the area now since I've been there."

"Sounds good," the Captain said. "Jim here did something like that, too. He was in Korea right after World War II; even studied some of the language."

"*Annyong hasimnikka*," Jim said with a laugh. "Don't try to use any more Korean than that with me. I've forgotten most of what I learned."

"I learned some, too," Jo said. "But in Korea they all spoke better Japanese than I did. Didn't really need any Korean."

Jo looked at the man — slightly round-faced, dark hair parted to one side, blue eyes which showed sincerity.

"Jim was asking how we got along with the Koreans, about the relationship between the U.S. soldiers — guys like us — and them," Jim said. "He's trying to weave what is happening today into some of his lectures."

"I got along fine with the Koreans," Jo said, "though I don't know about some of the other GIs. We had a common language — Japanese. Most of the GIs didn't. They'd refer to the Koreans as 'gooks,' maintained that the Koreans would steal anything they could get their hands on; that sort of thing. But if I were in the same situation as most of the Koreans are because of the war, I'd steal too."

"Know what you mean," Jim said. "Things were pretty bad even when I was there, before the Korean War." Then turning to the Captain, he asked, "How about you, Hobe? No language, no Asian background. Must've been harder."

"Not true," the Captain said. "I got along fine with them. I could tell by the way they smiled."

Jim nodded, though he may not have been convinced.

"I'm sure of what I say," the Captain said. After a pause, he leaned back; then looking first at Jim and then at Jo, said with an air of confidence, "You know, there's nothing like building international goodwill with the people-to-people diplomacy that Eisenhower is now talking about."

"Oh?" Jo said. He looked at the beer at the bottom of his glass, then over at Jim, and then at the Captain and asked, "By the way, that pond in our compound in Seoul, did you ever get any fish for it?"

Chapter Fourteen
Darlene

Living in London, Jo never thought of what it may have been like for ethnic Japanese living in Britain when Japan joined the other Axis powers in their war against the Allied forces and took Singapore and other areas of the British Empire. He met Darlene, though, and learned.

○

London in the early 1960's was new and exciting for Jo and his family. The English were supposed to be cold until they got to know you; the weather was supposed to be wet and foggy, and somehow he had thought that everyone would be speaking with the same BBC accent.

He found none of these things to be true. Jo and his wife thought London was wonderful, especially the people.

Then, there was also Darlene.

He first noticed her a few weeks after he, his wife and their three-year-old son had moved to the Kilburn area of Greater London. He caught a glimpse of her as she was getting onto the car ahead of him at the Kilburn High Road tube station during the early morning rush hour. He saw her only a second or so, but could see she was Eurasian — either half Japanese or half Chinese. His curiosity was aroused. Outside of his own family, there weren't many Asians around in the neighborhood.

A week or so later, he saw her again. With his son in a stroller, he was doing the weekend grocery shopping. His wife wanted some *sashimi*, so he had gone to the fishmonger first to see what was available. It was just a few minutes after 9 a.m. when the shops along the High Road had opened. Mackerel, cod, sole, flounder, eel, even some squid were neatly aligned on ice in separate trays on low, tilted platforms over the sawdust-covered floor.

"Look at the fishes' eyes to tell if they are fresh," his wife always said. Not seeing what he wanted, he was about to leave, when he saw some bream with pupils like clear gelatin, the convex lens wet and firm. Probably as fresh as could be expected. As he was inspecting the fish, he noticed out of the corner of his eyes that the Eurasian girl was standing on the sidewalk, her gaze intent on one of the trays.

Maybe she liked *sashimi*, too. He could tell her about the bream. *Sashimi* from bream was as good as the tuna you could buy in the Oriental food shops in Soho, or could eat at the Japanese restaurant on Leicester Square, and at about a third of the price.

But then, he thought, she might not know anything about *sashimi*. It would seem silly — he approaching a stranger in London and telling her, just because she looked half Asian, how good sea bream was, eaten raw.

He spotted her three or four times over the next week — getting on the tube train, out shopping, or merely passing by on the street. Though no words were exchanged nor eye contact made, she must have noticed him too. He thought of introducing himself, but then, didn't have to.

Jo had gone to the opening of a new Chinese restaurant off of St. James's Place in downtown London with Sayid, a Pakistani journalist friend. Other newsmen and women, embassy officials, business men, and people who simply knew the owner were invited.

The air in the crowded room was filled with the smell of steaming noodles, bean sprouts, roast pork, cooked ginger and soy sauce mixed with occasional whiffs of a woman's perfume or a man's after-shave lotion. Jo and Sayid had elbowed their way to the tables where the food was laid out and had filled their plates when Sayid looked up and saw someone he knew.

"You must meet her," he said. "You must. You have so much in common."

Jo looked up, and there with a half dozen Indian and Pakistani journalists who worked for BBC's overseas broadcast section was the Eurasian girl he had noticed in his neighborhood.

Her name was Darlene Matsushita — somehow the name Darlene didn't seem to fit. Sayid introduced Jo as "one of my best friends...of Japanese ancestry but actually an American."

"How nice," she said. "We meet quite a few Americans at BBC as well as Asians but you're the first Asian American I've met."

Jo liked her low-pitched voice, the English accent.

"I've seen you quite often in the Kilburn area," she continued. "Thought you might be Japanese. Now that I hear your accent, it's obvious you're from America. How do you like London?"

"Think it's great," Jo said.

"People say that," she said. "But I've lived here all my life. Have nowhere to compare it with."

He studied her face as she talked — a flat nose, brown Asian eyes, high cheek bones. Her hair, though, was reddish-brown and her skin showed some blotches of brown, something Jo had noticed before among other

Eurasians — as if the genes of the two races had not completely blended into an even mix. She seemed warm and friendly.

She worked on BBC's Asian desk, she explained; typed, proofread, handled correspondence. She liked her work, was interested in what was happening in the Orient, especially China and Japan, though, of course, BBC overseas broadcasts were aimed more at India, Pakistan and the other Asian Commonwealth countries.

"You can catch some BBC programs in Tokyo," Jo said.

"You've been in Tokyo, then?" she asked.

"Yeah."

"Oh, great," she said. "You've got to..." when Siddicki, one of the journalists, interrupted.

"Jo, what's the latest on the wire?" he asked. "Anything new on the Rann of Kutch?"

"Nothing new," Jo said, "doesn't seem to be a real crisis yet."

"But...," someone else said.

Jo looked back at Darlene; he would have liked to continue their conversation. She shrugged and smiled. When you are with Indian and Pakistani newsmen, you talk about India and Pakistan — Nehru, Ayub Khan, Kashmir, crises.

Some days later, Jo again saw Darlene on the platform at the tube station as he was on his way to work. She wore a tam, a green cloth coat trimmed with black fur, a red and green scarf, and shiny plastic boots appropriate for the chilly, damp weather. He saw her before she saw him, and in her expressionless face he again sensed a sadness — maybe a loneliness — he had sensed in her before.

Her face immediately brightened when she saw him, her smile erasing the signs of isolation from her face.

"I wanted to ask you more about Tokyo the other night," she said as they sat together after the train arrived.

"Where should I start?" Jo questioned.

"Did you see the TV documentary — 'The Two Faces of Japan'— for instance? Was it accurate?"

"As far as it went," Jo said. "But how much can you really say or show of a country in two half-hour programs?"

"The hot bathes, sleeping on the floor...*tatami*...I remember my father telling me," she said.

"That was the fun part," Jo said. "I felt much more comfortable living Japanese style when I was there."

"How about men?" she asked. "Is Japan that much a man's country?"

"In a way, though I knew some henpecked Japanese husbands," he said, thinking of Kagawa-san, a Japanese journalist Jo knew in Tokyo who always told his wife when he went out drinking, a wife who always hauled him home before he got too drunk and before he ran up too big a tab.

Darlene paused for a while, then tilting her head to one side, said, "While I watched, I wondered: how would it be for me to live there. The Japanese who come to BBC on exchange programs —

they've sent only men so far — hardly ever talk to me. They're as bad as some of the English men."

"Could be a language problem," Jo said.

"How would the Japanese in Japan see me?"

"It all depends," he said. "They'd be able to see that you are different. But try to learn their language, more about them. If your interest is genuine, they'd go out of their way to help; they'd love you."

"It might be fun living in Tokyo," she said. "It'll never happen, I know. But I'd like to go, even try to be one of them. Maybe I could feel like I belonged there. I'd like to feel like I belonged somewhere, anywhere, just once."

For the next two weeks, while Jo was still on the day shift, he saw Darlene almost every day as they went to work in the morning. He told her about New York, various other parts of the States, and Tokyo and other parts of Japan. She talked about trips to the Continent before the war, visits as a child to Kew Gardens, summer trips to Brighton. She mentioned her mother once or twice — "Mother still lives in Wimbledon," she said when Jo mentioned that when he and family first arrived in England they lived briefly at Tootin' Bec', just two tube stops away from the Wimbledon station. She mentioned two brothers, but said she rarely sees them.

During these conversations, Jo studied her face. Darlene was pleasant to look at, though not outstandingly pretty in the way he thought some of the Eurasian women he had known in New York and

Tokyo were. At times, in quiet moments, her face seemed like a mask hiding her emotions.

One morning, however, he got a glimpse of what he felt could be behind that mask. That morning the *London Daily Telegraph* had a picture of a burnt out tank in the fighting in the Congo, reminding Jo of pictures he had seen during World War II. He asked, somewhat casually, what had

happened to her family during the war.

"I and my brothers were moved out to the countryside with other children when the war started," she said. "Some of us even got gas masks. But then we were back in London by the time the real bombing started. In a way, it was an adventure for us. But poor Father."

She paused, remained silent for a moment, lost in her thoughts, then repeated, "Poor Father. It was hard on him, especially after Pearl Harbor and then the fall of Singapore."

Jo remained silent to let her continue.

"Being caught in between — I think that really broke his heart. Outside of work, he wouldn't leave the house for days. All of his Japanese friends were sent back to Japan. He wouldn't leave because of his family. We weren't much help either," she said. Her face seemed sadder than ever. "Mother and I, my brothers." Her father, she said, first learned his English in Japan, and though he lived in London for more than 20 years, never got rid of his "horrendous" accent until the day he died, though he tried so hard. No one in our family outside of him spoke any Japanese. "We listened but often there just seemed no way he could say all of what he wanted to say to us."

Darlene's face showed no tears, but for a moment her emotions seemed ready to surface.

What did her father do for a living? Jo was curious.

He was with a trading company, but, of course, that ended even before Pearl Harbor, she said. He began working part-time at BBC; used to broadcast in Japanese. He didn't want to do the broadcasts — wondered what his friends in Japan might think if they heard or even knew that he was broadcasting propaganda for the British. But he had to support his family.

"We could have all gotten permission to go with him if he returned to Japan," she said, "but he said, and we all felt, that there was no real choice but to stay here."

Jo could only look at the sadness on her face and wonder: being Japanese or half-Japanese in wartime London; what had it done to her?

For several weeks Jo was on the overnight shift at work and saw neither Darlene nor Sayid. But on the Monday when he started the dayside shift again, he saw Darlene as he boarded the tube train at Kilburn. She greeted him like a long-lost friend.

"Jo," she said once they were seated, "there's something I wanted to ask you, something I thought of since we last met. But now that you're here, I don't know quite how to start."

"I'll help if I can," Jo said.

"It's nothing I need. It's... Well, I don't know how you'll react."

"Me? Would it matter?" Jo asked.

"Oh yes," she said. "Except for Father, you're the only Japanese — Japanese American or any sort of Japanese — I've really talked to. You won't be upset?"

"You still haven't told me what you're going to ask?"

"Well...," she said, "my surname, Matsushita. It does mean pine tree or something of that nature, doesn't it?"

"Yeah," he said, though he thought she already knew. "It's a place name — means 'beyond the pines,' 'under the pines,' or something like that. That's how a lot of Japanese names came about, by a family's location. Why?"

"I've been thinking about it," she said, then looked across the aisle as she searched for her words. The other passengers in the car seemed almost as drab as the weather outside. Men with bowler hats, striped pants and umbrellas were mixed with others in heavy coats and rubber boots. The slim softness of the younger women was hidden by overcoats, scarves, and woolen hats. As Jo waited for Darlene to continue he also was aware of the hissing and the warmth of the radiator pipe by his feet, the stuffiness of the closed air, and the smell of rubberized raincoats.

"I haven't told you about it yet, have I?" she finally said — she was still looking across the aisle and spoke slowly. "My brothers, both of them, changed their names during to war to 'Pine.' 'Matsushita' is so hard for the English to say, they said."

"So?" Jo asked.

"I'm thinking about doing the same," she said; then, immediately looking directly into Jo's face, asked, maybe pleaded, "It would be all right, wouldn't it?"

Change her name? He grew up with people who Westernized their given names: "Carl" for "Kazuo," "Kenneth" for "Kenichi," "Mary" for "Mari," or "Heidi" for "Hideko." Even his own name,

"Joji," was shortened to "Jo" by those who knew him, though it could have been even more Westernized by making it "Joe." But a surname?

"It would be all right, wouldn't it?" she repeated.

"Oh, sure...sure," Jo said.

"I'm so glad you agree with me," she said. Then, as she reached and touched his hand, she said, "I knew you would understand."

Jo wasn't quite sure of how he felt — disappointed, maybe — as he got off the train at the Temple Inn station and began walking toward his office. What Darlene had said still churned in his mind, though she, when she had gotten off at an earlier stop, seemed happily reassured. Of course, it wasn't the first time anyone had changed a surname, he told himself. It happened all the time in America. Maybe it was just a matter of convenience. "Matsushita," even if the spelling was phonetic, still was difficult for English speakers to pronounce. Darlene would have another name if she got married. If she was trying to hide an identity, why do it after all these years? Why didn't she do it when her brothers did? What difference should it make to him, anyway?

But he remained disappointed. Was it the war? The sadness he sensed in her seemed even more prevailing.

The walk to the office took Jo through a terraced garden, now brown and covered with soggy leaves, into the courtyard of the Temple Church with its shallow, cone-shaped steeple. A plaque identified the church as the starting point for the crusades of the Knights of Templar. From the courtyard, he walked under some high oaks which seemed old enough to have been planted about the time the church was built. Beyond the trees, Jo went by the Law Courts with halls and buildings still in use after a hundred years.

Walking by the old structures gave Jo a feeling of the continuity of things and people. This helped put things into perspective. How many hundreds of thousands of people had walked through this place over the centuries? he wondered. How many massive events of history occurred while the buildings and trees remained unchanged?

Darlene changing her name — did it matter that much?

Chapter Fifteen
A Penny For The Guy

America has Halloween, Britain has "Guy Fawkes Night."

O

The air was damp as Jo stepped out of his flat, shopping bag in hand, onto the short pathway to the sidewalk, and down Exeter Road toward the bus stop by the Kilburn tube station. It hadn't rained since Jo left the local pub the night before, but the pathway was wet; dew dripped from the hedge, and the broad leaves from maple trees along the street made a soggy, slippery carpet.

Better get more pennies, Jo thought as he joined the queue at the bus stop. In the evening it would be Guy Fawkes Night; kids would be collecting pennies for their "Guy."

When Jo and his family had first arrived and moved into the flat in the northwest part of Greater London, he was surprised by kids on the streets seemingly begging. Then people explained that Guy Fawkes Night was a traditional thing, a little like Halloween in America. The pennies the kids asked for were for firecrackers, sparklers, roman candles and other fireworks to be set off November 5, the anniversary of the Guy Fawkes' attempt to blow up the Houses of Parliament.

There'd be the bonfires in people's backyards and the fireworks on the Thames, too, Jo was thinking, when a friendly voice behind him asked, "How's your head?"

"Oh, hello," Jo said when he turned and recognized the woman who ran a greengrocers in the neighborhood.

"My brother told me he met you at the North Star last night."

"Yeah, we had quite a few," Jo acknowledged. "But I feel fine. How's Desmond."

"A bit under the weather, but not too bad," she said. "Does him good to do it occasionally."

Jo nodded. Desmond, her brother, worked all day at the Smith Motor Parts plant up the road, but helped her and her two daughters run the greengrocers on weekends.

"Where you going to shop in this weather?" she asked.

"Portobello Road. Wife wants some Chinese cabbage, white radishes, squid, things we can't find on the High Road here. But I like the bus ride and don't mind the weather at all."

"You must be getting used to our weather by now anyway," she said. "You've been here how long now? Six? Seven years?"

"Eight," Jo said. "We came in 1960. It's already 1968."

"Well, you're practically a Londoner. No, you are a Londoner now," she said. "You've become one of us. No wonder you just shrug off this weather."

"Could be," Jo smiled. She was about his own age — in her mid-forties, red hair turning gray, body plump.

"I remember when you and your family first came to our greengrocers," she said. "Your son in the pram; cute, like an Oriental doll, he was."

"Yeah," Jo said as a No.9A bus — a large double decker — came lumbering down the High Road, the gaudy advertisements on its sides highlighted by its bright red paint. It was his bus.

As Jo went up to the top deck of the bus, he thought of what the woman had said, felt flattered that she insisted that he was now a Londoner.

The night before, when he had come in from the cold, the saloon bar at the North Star had seemed particularly warm and inviting. People were two or three deep around the horseshoe-shaped bar, half with their coats on, more out of habit than because they were cold. Above the hum of voices and occasional loud laughter, Jo heard the shouts — "two pints coming up," "whiskey here, Gov," or "that'll be six shillings, please."

"Hey Jo, over here," came a voice.

"There you are," Jo said wiping away the fog that had formed on his glasses. Desmond and a half dozen others sat on stools at the far end of the bar, forming a semi-circle.

"What'll you have?" Desmond asked.

"A Guinness, what else."

"A half? A pint?"

"Make it a pint," Jo said. "I'm way behind you people tonight."

"You like your Guinness, don't you," Desmond said as the beer arrived. "I'll have to take you with me the next time I go home to Dublin. They really know how to pour it there, not like these English."

"What'd you think of the 'Spurs the other night?" Frank interrupted.

"Mean Greaves?"

"They're others on the team, you know," Frank said.

"Yeah. But it was Greaves who scored the 'hat trick,'" someone else countered.

"Jo," Desmond said, turning away from the sports discussion, "before you came in we were discussing the series of articles in the Daily Mail about the racial stuff in America by this guy — what's his name, Mulchrone? Anyway, what'd you think?"

"Articles seem fair enough," Jo said. "Mulchrone's a pretty good writer."

"He seems to be good," Desmond acknowledged. "But what I want to ask is what you think about what's happening in America. The blacks and whites, can't they get along? You're a Yank; maybe you know."

"Hell, I don't know," Jo sighed. "Haven't been home for years."

Jo could see a frown on Desmond's face as he talked. Desmond had a round face with an extra light complexion, black but thinning hair, and a slight moustache. He was a bit heavy set and reminded Jo of Hardy in the old Laurel and Hardy films.

"Bloody bastards..." Desmond mumbled. "Why?"

Jo shook his head and sipped his beer. "Bloody bastards, Bloody Yanks" — Desmond used the terms, so did Frank, so did the others.

"You know, I'm not being personal when I call Americans 'bloody bastards,'" Desmond said, "especially in your case."

"Sure," Jo said, "sure."

"Don't know why I'm getting on your back," Desmond said. "Took me a long time to even think of you as a Yank. Bet most people in London still don't. You're not black or white. We know better, but most people here keep thinking all Yanks have to be one or the other, or maybe one of your Red Indians."

Jo shrugged.

"Remember?" Desmond asked. "Remember when I first met you here?"

"Yeah."

"You were standing in line at the bar waiting to order a drink," Desmond said. "Thought you must have come from China or Japan. You were so damn polite and reserved. I had to yell at Louie behind the bar to get his attention or you would never have gotten served. Never would've thought of you as a bloody Yank until I heard you order a Guinness with that accent of yours.

149

But getting back to this racial stuff in America, it upsets me completely. Hell, I'm Irish. I like America; what it stands for. My father — he's dead now, died in the war — was going to go to America before he changed his mind and came to London instead. Got relatives in Boston, New York, all over the place. But all this violence... They just shot this black man, Martin Luther...uh..."

"...King, Jr.," Jo said.

"Now they've shot Bobby Kennedy. What's happening?"

Jo looked at the foam on top of the dark beer that filled half of his mug as he collected his thoughts. America — the riots, civil rights, peace marches, student unrest — things were changing.

"I don't know," Jo finally said. "I'm in the news business; see a lot of stuff that never even gets into the papers here. But I'm not home; I'm not part of what's going on there. Maybe I should go back, experience it myself."

"Ah, come on Jo, you're one of those bloody bastards; you're a bloody Yank," Frank broke in again. "You're all bloody bastards. But I don't give a damn. Hurry and finish that drink so I can order another round. They're short of mugs here."

With that everyone started to laugh.

"Oh, the Hell with you, Frank," Jo said, then gulping down the rest of his beer, joined the laughter.

"Hey, Desmond, what's this about new procedures in the stock room at the plant," Ted, another member of the group, asked. He and others of the group worked with Desmond at the auto parts plant where Desmond was one of the union stewards.

"Relax. See me tomorrow. I'll take it up then, at the shop, not here," Desmond said.

The beer kept coming. The talk became more disorganized. Soon, Jo was not sure of who was talking about what. The discussion never got back to America and its racial problems.

Jo walked part of the way toward his flat with Desmond after the pub closed.

"You don't mind all the joking and needling you get when you're with us, do you?" Desmond asked. "I could stop it all if you want."

"Naw. Doesn't bother me at all; not at all," Jo said truthfully.

O

Jo was quite pleased as he made his way back from Portobello Road to the bus stop near the Paddington Station where he had gotten off the 9A bus earlier. He'd bought the cabbage and radishes his wife wanted, but better yet, he had found some fresh octopus at the fishmonger. He, his wife and son had been invited to the MacKays for the evening to watch the fireworks and bonfire. The MacKays had often asked about Japanese food, something different. He would surprise them with cooked octopus.

Jo was thinking about where could he buy some fireworks to take along as well, when he noticed three boys — about 9 or 10 years old — down the street with their "Guy."

Good, he thought, he had a pocket full of change.

"A penny for the Guy?" one of the boys asked as Jo approached.

"Sure thing," Jo said as he put his shopping bag down and reached into his pocket. Their "Guy" looked fairly good — an old pin-striped suit and a torn, white shirt, stuffed with straw; cotton gloves for hands, and a mustachioed face drawn on the remains of white hosiery, all topped by a tattered gray felt hat. The effigy of the renegade was propped up in a red wagon against a low cast iron fence along the sidewalk.

Jo was about to compliment the boy on his "Guy" when the boy suddenly said in an exaggerated singsong voice, "Ah so, Chinee likee flier-clackie, too."

Jo could see the boy's eyes; the half-snickering, half-snide smile on the pinched-up face. The other two boys laughed in approval.

Jo felt a flush of anger over the crude mockery, dropped the coins in his hand back into his pocket.

"Sorry," Jo told the surprised boy, and walked on.

Only 10-year-olds, shouldn't get annoyed, Jo said to himself as he walked, almost reaching the bus stop before his anger cooled. Probably didn't know any better, just reflecting the sentiments of their parents or people of the neighborhood. "A Londoner...one of us," the lady from the greengrocers had said.

But stuck fast in the back of Jo's mind was a ditty he had heard when he was about 10 years old himself, attending grade school in California. The ditty started out, "Ching Chong Chinaman..."

Author with the sugar beet gang and owner, Mr. Glantz, in the sugar beet fields outside of Billings, Montana, Fall, 1942.

Chapter Sixteen
Bernice

February 18, 1999 — The Justice Department closed the books this week on a $1.6 billion reparations program for ethnic Japanese interned in American camps during World War II.... The redress program made $20,000 payments to Japanese Americans or their heir – DEMOCRACY NOW, The War and Peace Report

O

"Bernice," the young girl said. "My grandmother's maiden name was Bernice Peterson. I was asked to look for you because she thought you might be here."

"Bernice?" For Jo (short of Joji) the name didn't immediately ring a bell.

"Santa Clara High School, class of '41," the girl said. Her eyes brightened. "I got excited when I saw your name, Joji Kono, on the list of names of those attending this camp reunion. Embarrassing, but I kept looking at name tags as men were passing. Finally, I've found you."

"Oh?" Jo said, surprised. He had noticed the girl as she approached – blonde hair, blue-eyed, pale skin. There were other Caucasian faces, some obviously of mixed blood, among those of Japanese ancestry attending the "Camp Reunion."

"My grandmother and you were classmates in high school," the young girl went on. "Then she used to see you at San Jose State before the war broke out. She was one of five sisters, all with names starting with 'B.' Beatrice was a sister two years younger, who also attended Santa Clara when you two did."

"Bernice?" Jo shook his head. His memory was blank. The year was 1997. Class of '41 — high school, San Jose State, the war, the camps — more than a half century ago.

As Jo shook his head, the young girl continued, "Grandma said she and you were in a lot of classes together at what was then Santa Clara Union High School — trigonometry, solid geometry, physics, Latin II — only six were in your Latin II class. Grandma said after they moved the people out of California you used to write to her."

Jo still shook his head.

"Anyway, my name is Denise," the girl continued, still smiling though possibly hiding a let down. "Here, while I'm at it, let me introduce you. This is my husband, Karl — short for Kaoru — Karl Inouye. We've been married for two years now."

"Well, congratulations," Jo said, shaking the young man's hand. Karl was what would be known in Japanese as a *Yonsei*, a fourth generation Japanese American. "There were several Inouye families in and around Mountain View, Sunnyvale, Santa Clara. I could have known your grandparents."

"Could have," the youngster nodded. "I'll ask Grandma. We came with her. She was in Heart Mountain, too. I'll introduce you later when I find her. She still lives near Santa Clara. Maybe you even knew her."

"Could have," Jo nodded.

"But please, please," the young girl broke in. "Try to remember my grandma. It'll mean so much to her. There's something she feels you've got to know."

As the young couple moved away, Jo wondered, "Got to know?" He tried to recall the name. But high school, college, 1941-'42? His sister could be of no help, she started Santa Clara High the year after he had graduated, and obviously, neither could his wife, who was born and grew up in Shanghai before coming to the United States in 1948 shortly after the war. Latin II, physics, trigonometry – the classes were all small — then San Jose State. Bernice? The disappointment on the young girl's face stuck in the back of his mind.

Bernice Peterson? Who was she? How did it happen that he'd get a message from her at this reunion of Japanese Americans who had been incarcerated during World War II? "Camp Reunions" was what they are called. These "Camps" themselves were unique; ten such camps were set up during World War II in remote mountain areas of the West to house Japanese Americans – be they citizens or not – who were forcibly removed from homes in the U.S. West Coast. Some called them "concentration camps," which, in a sense, they were.

The reunions of internees of the various "Relocation Centers," as they were officially called, didn't start taking place until forty or fifty years after the war. Other reunions— of high school or college classes, military units, certain battle or campaign experiences shared during WWII and Korea – usually had begun long ago, many had already come and gone as people of that era passed away. Could be that those who had been in camps were too busy putting their lives together afterwards to think of reunions, maybe it just took a long time for people to get around to marking or celebrating what for most had been a traumatic change in their lives.

The particular camp reunion Jo was attending with his wife and sister was being held in Seattle in the fall of 1997. It was organized by people (and their relatives, mainly sons, daughters and grandchildren) who had been interned at the camp at Heart Mountain, Wyoming. The camp site was in the northwestern corner of Wyoming, not too far from Yellowstone National Park, though the site itself had little in common with the scenic splendors of Yellowstone. (Maps showed the particular peak the camp was supposed to be named after was not "Heart Mountain" but "Harte Mountain," honoring an early American explorer of the area. Somehow, maybe to give it a romantic air, the camp name officially became "Heart Mountain.")

Jo was attending this reunion with his wife and a younger sister mainly because his sister wanted to attend, meet some of those she had attended high school with in the camp. Jo, now retired, was at the reunion mainly because his sister, who flew in from Hawaii, had asked him to be there.

His wife, of Chinese descent who came to America after World War II, wanted to experience what she could of his background. She also would have a chance to see to a close friend, someone who had been a classmate in Shanghai and now lived in the Seattle area. As an added incentive, they could visit Jo's other younger sister's daughter, who lived in Seattle. That younger sister though, who was still in the fourth and fifth grades in camp and now lived in upstate New York, didn't have the slightest interest in attending the camp reunion.

Jo originally was not all that enthused either about attending the reunion, but felt it could be fun meeting those he had gone to grammar school and high school with but had not seen or knew anything about since the camp days.

Signing in at this Heart Mountain reunion followed a pattern he had become familiar with while attending other conferences — though more often as a news wire reporter rather than an attendee — sign-in desks, programs and other handouts, old photos, letters, news clippings.

It was still the first day of the reunion when the young girl approached him. Bernice? Santa Clara High School? San Jose State? How'd it tie in with this camp reunion? He forced his mind to go back, to try to recall.

Santa Clara, in the pre-World War II days before people had even dreamed of such things as computer chips, was known for, among other things, the University of Santa Clara which used to produce good football teams, and the Mission Santa Clara, established by the Spanish missionaries who accompanied the Conquistadores in the late 1700's. The original natives of the area, a small primitive tribe known as Digger Indians, had become extinct not too long after the arrival of the Spanish missionaries.

But Santa Clara then also was known locally as a "cannery town" where Libby's, California Canning Company (CCC), and others processed and canned the fruits and vegetables produced in the nearby countryside. Prune, pear, walnut, apricot, cherry and peach orchards; dairy farms, raspberry and strawberry patches, and a handful of truck garden farms dominated that area of Santa Clara Valley, which, before WWII, proudly proclaimed itself the "Prune Capital of the World."

Of the graduating 121 students in June, 1941 from Santa Clara Union High School, one girl went on to Stanford, one boy to the University of California in Berkeley; another girl said she was going to the University of Oregon, but she wasn't very smart and didn't have the grades so Jo always doubted she would have ever gotten there. The others from the class who were college-bound, about a dozen or so, went to what was then still San Jose State College, the closest and least expensive of the colleges in the surrounding area. One or two could have gone to the University of Santa Clara, Jo didn't know.

San Jose State? He remembered two other pre-engineering students from Santa Clara in his calculus and physics classes, and seeing a few of the others from his high school class on the campus at San Jose State. But the name Bernice still did not ring a bell. Of course, after WWII and the GI Bill many more would have gone on to higher education.

As he pondered over the name, he heard someone call, "Hey Sarge" but didn't pay any attention – the Army, Japan, Korea – that was so long ago.

"Hey," the voice insisted, and then he felt a hand from the back on his shoulders.

As Jo turned, there was instant recognition.

"Sasai," Jo said. "Hell, I didn't even know you were at Heart Mountain." Sasai, a draftee, joined him in the spring of 1952 on the three-man editing staff in Seoul of the Eighth Army interrogation team. Their job was to edit PW interrogation reports from teams at the main PW station in Yong Dong Po, just north across the river from Seoul, and from others with the headquarters of various regiments and divisions along the front lines. Sasai was an opera fan (his mother, he said, loved opera and took him along when he was a child) and, after several beers he would often burst into arias, especially from "Madame Butterfly." All the time they worked and drank together in Seoul, neither, however, ever mentioned having been in the Heart Mountain camp though Sasai would have been in the camp school, probably at the same grade level as one or the other of Jo's younger sisters.

Sasai mentioned several others who had been at Berkeley under Korean GI Bill – Henderson, who had been in Korea as a child with his missionary parents; Ueda, another co-editor; Kim, born in Shanghai and speaking Chinese rather than Korean in spite of his ancestry, who ended up with the U. S. State Department.

There were short introductions – Sasai introduced his wife, who was born and raised in Japan, someone Sasai was introduced to for a family-arranged marriage. Jo and Sasai promised to see each other later to talk about old times as they parted.

In the main reception room where a "Get Together" was set to renew old acquaintances, Jo, his wife and his sister met several others Jo hadn't seen for years. His sister-in-law's sister and her husband, who Jo last met in Tokyo just before Jo was shipped to Korea, were there with two grown daughters. He saw a middle aged woman he thought was Nobuko, one of the girls from the neighboring Nakamoto family in Mountain View when Jo's family first moved to that area from Bacon Island in the San Joaquin River delta area. But "No," the woman said, "Buki died several years ago, I'm one of the younger sisters."

The one daughter and one of the younger sons of the Shimada's, a family of eight brothers and one sister who grew strawberries on rented land not far from Jo's own family farm, stopped to say "Hello." Jo remembered the girl riding on the same high school bus though he couldn't remember ever talking to her. One of the brothers was on the high school wrestling team with Jo. Several other people were familiar. He noticed as he greeted those he had not seen for years that as they approached, they looked old, i.e. their age, but once he recognized who they were they seemed to look no different than they did when teenagers so long ago.

Walking about the main reception room, the disappointment that showed on the face of the young girl when he couldn't remember her grandmother was still lingering in his mind when he approached a man being pushed in a wheel chair.

It was Tad, short for Tadao, who along with his older brother George, was part of an eight-man crew who had gone outside of camp in the fall of 1942, a month or so after their arrival at Heart Mountain, to top sugar beets on a farm outside of Billings, Montana. The internees at the Heart Mountain camp were called on to do their "patriotic duty" to go out of the barbed-wired enclosures to help save the sugar beet crop in neighboring Rocky Mountain areas. Though the eight-man crew Jo was with returned to camp with about $80 each after a month and a half of back-breaking work (the beets on the farm were small) it at least got them out of camp. The woman pushing the wheel chair was Tad's wife, also from Japan through an arranged marriage. Tad's folks and hers were from the same village in Fukuoka in southern Japan. Before the war, Tad and his family lived in Cupertino and went to the same Japanese-American Methodist church outside of Mountain View that Jo's family attended.

Later, when the team returned to camp Tad became one of the 59 so-called "draft resisters" who did not foreswear loyalty to the United States but also refused to be inducted into the military until their civil rights were restored. Tad, always a good student, was standing up for his rights as he was told in school he should always do, and after having taken a stand on his basic right as an American, had to live with a stigma attached to him by some fellow Nisei, i.e. particularly those who were so anxious to be considered Americans that they went along with whatever the white majority said. These Nisei, Jo felt, somehow didn't consider themselves American enough and went out of their way to prove that they were, inadvertently adding a bit of credence in a backhanded way to the then often repeated assertion of "Once a Jap, always of Jap" by the then commander of the U.S. West Coast Defense Command.

Jo, born in Tokyo, was automatically denied citizenship and did not have to make any choice at that time. But he could sense the turmoil that must have gone through the minds of his friends; those who decided to stand up and resist the further taking away of what was always the basic rights of all Americans..

The 59 draft resisters served two years in federal prison before being pardoned after the war by President Truman. Two others of the same eight-man sugar beet crew also took the same stand. However, Tad's older brother Ichiro, who was with the same beet-topping team, was drafted from camp, went through the military intelligence school to learn Japanese and ended up in the Pacific during the war.

Jo was aware of what had happened to Tad and the other draft resisters, but Jo made no mention of that, instead asked about and was told that Ichiro had passed away several years back, that a sister Jo knew was still living in Honolulu.

As the two were reminiscing, Tad asked, "Remember the girl you used to write to when we were in Billings? What was her name – Bernice, Bernice

Peterson? Anyway, her granddaughter is here, married a kid from the Inouye family — you know the family that lived on the farm not too far from the Jefferson Elementary School."

"Oh," Jo reacted. Tad's mention of Billings and the letters he was then writing and receiving, immediately brought back memories half forgotten over the years. Like the opening of the locks of a mental dam, memories of people, events, the wholesale change of the family's life and fortune during the months after the Japanese attack on Pearl Harbor came back in torrents.

Bernice, he remembered her face — she wore very little make-up, had pale skin that somehow seemed to reflect her very quiet nature; she was taller than he, about five feet seven or eight; slim, had brownish-blonde hair. He never thought of her as pretty or not pretty, but as a friend, someone he was always happy to see.

Throughout his high school days, he had never even thought of dating anyone, not even the Nisei girls in his classes let alone dating Bernice. In 1941, not too many of the students at Santa Clara even thought of going on to college (though after World War II and the subsequent GI Bill Jo was sure many more would have gone on to higher education). Only about a dozen or so students in their senior class were taking pre-college courses. Bernice was in his Latin I and Latin II classes, the latter which had only six students; in the same English 4, physics, solid geometry and trigonometry classes. When at San Jose State, he and she often sat at the same desk in the reading room of the then new library. He didn't have the slightest memory of what they may have talked about or even if they talked that much at all.

The days following the Japanese attack on Pearl Harbor, things were hectic for everyone. Who knew? Was there going to be a Japanese attack on the Pacific Coast? There was a general blackout at night; men in the reserves were being called up; the drafting of men into the Army had begun some time before, now volunteers were flooding the recruiting stations.

Suspects – German, Italian or Japanese — were being picked up and sent away; to where, even their families weren't told. In the Japanese communities things reached the stage of panic in some families – he remembered the father of a family with ten children castrating himself; another man took rat poison. Teachers at the Japanese language schools, leaders of Japanese community organizations, people who one way or another seemed a community leader were arrested by newly- designated deputy sheriffs or deputized FBI agents..

At school, Jo used to eat his bread and butter sandwiches with eight or nine other pre-engineering students who gathered on a bench outside the lecture hall after the 11 a.m. pre-engineering physics lecture. He listened, but never did much talking. They knew who he was, though, because they were in many classes together, and in math and physics, for instance, scores after each examination were posted on the class bulletin boards.

After Pearl Harbor, the conversation within the group as they ate lunch was about who was in the reserves and being called up, who was taking their physical for the draft, who volunteered, what was being done with newly-imposed gasoline and sugar rations, bond drives, victory gardens, etc. Jo remembered one of the students, talking proudly about growing red radishes in the family garden at home, part of the patriotic push for home gardening after the start of the war. Jo's family were truck-garden farmers; he couldn't help but think: little red radishes – like they'd fulfill a family's needs for fresh vegetables?

Jo usually said little as he sat with the group. No one said anything to him about the war and he being Japanese. There were no snide remarks. But Jo felt uncomfortable. He soon drifted away from the lunch group, eating his sandwiches alone on a second-story walkway over the main campus quad. His brother, who was two years ahead of him, also brought his lunch and sat with a group of Nisei but Jo never joined that group either.

He remembered a Dr. Meyer, the calculus professor. Dr. Meyer was a reserve officer, one of the first to be called up after Pearl Harbor, but then he returned to the campus because he failed to pass his physical. As Jo stood alone, the professor happened to be passing by, put his hand on Jo's shoulder, simply said, "Keep your chin up." It was a simple gesture but Jo never forgot the genuine warmth of the professor's action.

Other memories returned. He remembered upsetting his father. His father was extra jittery after the war started. Though their farm was out in the rural area, his father was jittery, afraid that he too might be picked up as were others of the Japanese American community and sent off, to where, even their families did not know. His father's nervousness showed when Jo, once during the numerous blackouts on the West Coast that December, raised the shade of a living room window just a bit – blackout sirens had just sounded. Jo wanted to see if all the neighboring farm houses were obeying the signal. His father, without a word, pushed him aside, pulled the shade down.

Jo remembered the wild rumors – Japanese warships off the West Coast, claimed signals from Japanese spies within the local community, furrows in farm fields indicating directions of major U.S. military installations; other stories were circulated in the press though it mattered to no one that such reports later prove to be completely false. All sorts of rumors also circulated on what should or would happen to the local Japanese families until official notice finally came out – anyone with any Japanese blood would have to leave the Western Defense Command area – which included most of California, Oregon, Washington, and parts of Arizona. Life then changed.

The farm Jo's family lived on was nominally partly theirs (about 14 acres out of 40 or so), the rest their neighbors, but once the evacuation orders were announced, the separated acreages were united and the land prepared for sugar beets, which became an essential national defense crop. Jo's older brother, who was finishing up his Batchelor's degree at Berkeley, returned home to help with the preparations for evacuation. Jo and his next older brother drove to school after Japanese were barred from taking the local train and stayed enrolled in school at San Jose State until almost the end of the spring quarter when the orders for all ethnic Japanese to leave their homes were finally issued by the Western Army Defense Command.

While Jo remained in school he continued to meet Bernice at the library. What they talked about, he couldn't remember. Why they decided to write to each other when he knew he would have to leave, he couldn't remember either. Did he ask, or did she ask? But write they did.

While he and his family were at the Santa Anita racetrack where a temporary "assembly center" was set up Jo wrote to Bernice of the horse stable they were housed in – a neighboring stable had a star on the door and rumor had it that it was the stall used by the famed "Sea Biscuit." The family slept on canvas bag filled with straw which the internees gathered from piles dumped at the corners of the row of stables. Those assigned to the stables often voiced complaints of the smell in the stables in spite of the lime spread over the asphalt floors to hide the odor..

When the bulk of those from the Santa Clara and San Jose areas had arrived at Santa Anita, a new category of work was assigned — those who were native born and thus U.S. citizens were drafted to work to make camouflage nets. Jo, born in Tokyo, was not a citizen, could not work on the nets, and since most of the other jobs at the center – mess hall help, garbage collectors, camp police, office help – were all filled, had time to try to keep up with his math and physics, other engineering courses, had time to do much of what he felt he should have. But, instead, for the first time in his life, spent most of that summer loafing; went to a judo class; even took some dancing lessons.

He wrote to Bernice about his life-of-Riley type existence, of the food some complained about, but for him seemed quite adequate. Many of the interns complained about too many meals of wieners and sour kraut, powdered milk, watery mashed potatoes, little change in menu. But for Jo, who grew up during the "Great Depression" of the 1930's, the food seemed quite adequate.

At night in Santa Anita, search lights flashed around all areas of the camp, armed guards stood in watch towers. Jo remembered writing to Bernice about a scene when he and his family first arrived at Santa Anita and were having their baggage inspected. An old man in line ahead of them tried to sneak in a bottle of Johnny Walker wrapped in clothing at the bottom of a suit case. The man merely showed chagrin on being caught when the bottle was taken away; his teenaged daughter's face was red with embarrassment; the mother bowed apologetically at the guard before scurrying through.

Several weeks after Jo's family's arrival at Santa Anita, the more or less calm that had been prevailing, was broken. Trouble started in the "Blue Mess" (different mess halls in the various areas of the camp were designated by color). An inmate worker there was unhappy with his boss, a *hakujn* hired from outside the camp as a supervisor. The internee threw a coffee mug at the white man, why – it was never quite clear. But soon loud sirens blared over the camp loudspeaker system; then soldiers came marching in through the front gate.

Jo remembered writing to Bernice about watching the soldiers: "They were office types, nervous, hardly able to stand properly in formation," he wrote. He also told of the mass rush later to the grandstand at the main race track where a general meeting was being held after the start of the incident; people trampling over miniature gardens so tenderly cared for which had been started in front of some of the barracks, of several people speaking before the gathered crowd, though he couldn't recall what was said.

Bernice almost always answered the letters he wrote in a week or two. She wrote about what was happening with those both knew. Mrs. Livingston, their freshman algebra and sophomore geometry teacher was called up. She was a WAC captain in the reserves. Don Johnson, a classmate who joined the Navy immediately after graduation was at Pearl Harbor when the Japanese attacked. Pat Boosie, in their Latin class and a majorette in the school band, married one of the stars on the high school football team before the man went into the Navy and off to boot camp.

Once Jo's family arrived at Heart Mountain, Jo wrote of the ten-day long train ride through the heat of the Mojave desert, the picturesque rout along a river through the Rockies; seeing antelope on the open grassland of the Rocky Mountains, and then the arrival at the camp itself in Wyoming. Along the way, their train constantly had to be side-tracked for trains carrying troops and military equipment in the opposite direction.

Preparation of the camp site had not quite been finished when the evacuees arrived, and six men from among the evacuees themselves were recruited to finish putting up the barbed wire around the camp. Jo wrote to Bernice about youngsters from the families in the barracks along the edge of the camp throwing stones at their fellow evacuees assigned to finish putting up the barbed wire and had to be replaced by Caucasian laborers from farms around nearby Cody and Powell.

Jo got a job in camp shoveling coal out of box cars onto trucks for the pop-bellied stoves that heated the barracks (a job he took because he then had to work only four hours a day), then later was with the eight-man sugar beet-topping crew to Montana when he last wrote to Bernice. She was working at one of the local canneries in Santa Clara, wrote about an accident, losing some of her fingers. He wrote back expressing his sympathy. But after that he never heard back from her again. For a long time, he was bothered by the thought that maybe he had said something wrong in his last letter to her though he could not think of anything he may have said that would have offended her. Eventually, he completely forgot about her.

At the reunion when Mits brought back his memory of Bernice, there was a moment of deep chagrin. He had to find the young *hakujin* girl who had talked to him earlier about her grandmother; found her and her husband as the conferees were gathering that evening for the formal conference supper.

"Grandma's mother, when she found out her daughter was writing to you in camp, ordered her to stop," the granddaughter said. "Her mother thought it was wrong that her daughter was writing to anyone Japanese. Grandma said she never felt so bad after being ordered not to write to you. But her mother could see you only as a Japanese, one of the enemy."

"Oh!" Jo reacted. Momentarily his emotions surged – not with anger but with the memory of the helplessness he felt at the time of how so many in America looked on him and his people at the start of the war. The concern over why Bernice had stopped writing, something he tried not to acknowledge but could not help but nurse for so many years, was remembered and now finally lifted. He wanted to hug and kiss the young girl for the information she conveyed, but of course he didn't, it would have not have been Japanese-like; it also may have embarrassed her.

He got Bernice's married name, her address, promised to write to her. But even as he did, he wondered, "What could I write about after 50 years?"

As he left the girl and her *Yonsei* husband to return to his table, he knew that America's younger generation in some ways was more grown up than his own World War II contemporaries.

Epilogue

Life: ...the sequence of physical and mental experiences that make up the existence of an individual... "Webster's New Collegiate Dictionary"

O

Father would have liked the simple ceremony at the cemetery where his ashes were being interred.

The group was small, just family and a few friends. Jo's father was 92 years old when he died; Jo's mother had passed away a short year and a half before. None of his father's personal friends were there; all already having died or living far away from New York. The weather was warm for late October; leaves had turned to varying shades of yellow, orange and red, though non-conifers still showed a bit of green along with the pines and cedars.

Jo did not grieve, though tears glistened in the eyes of others as his oldest brother spoke. Jo had talked to his father six months earlier in Honolulu. Despite his age, his father was healthy and still lucid. He admitted, though, having difficulty remembering things. With Mother and all of those he knew gone, father had made it plain that he felt it was time for him to go as well.

The cemetery, in Hartsdale just north of New York City, had only name plates which lay flat on the ground to mark each grave along its hillsides. His father's grave was next to that of Mother's. It seemed appropriate that their final resting place was on the opposite side of the world from their native villages in Japan.

Father was of that generation in a Japan that took its cues from the West, especially America, and was hell-bent on catching up. The West inspired ambitions that spurred that generation on. Young men of that time sought horizons that reached far beyond the confines of the Japanese islands. Though America had material wealth, that was not the main reason for his father leaving Japan. The underlying lure for him was a strong desire to experience what America was, a nation of nations.

His father and mother visited Japan several times after the end of the war. For them, though, it was a Japan that was no longer home. In the cemeteries of each of their villages — Mother's in Saitama and Father's in a remote area high up in the southern Japan Alps — they had family plots.

But neither ever expressed any desire of being buried anywhere excepting in America. Their names and that of their children have been crossed off of the family register in Father's native village.

Jo and his two brothers took turns shoveling the loose soil over the square brass urn holding their father's ashes.

Jo's wife, his children; his niece and her husband, their children; the son of the family where Jo's mother and father were employed for so many years in the later part of the working lives; friends from his brother's school — all were watching as soil was shoveled to cover the urn.

As he helped bury the urn, Jo thought of the times he had watched his father plant black walnuts in the orchard on their farm. The nuts sprouted and grew, and in a few years the saplings became the sturdy stock on which English walnuts were grafted.

Similarly, his mother and father's transplanted family now seemed part of America's stock for the future.

○

Jo was on temporary duty in San Francisco from Washington, D.C. and saw Angel Island, the Ellis Island of the West Coast, while riding the ferry from Larkspur Landing in Marin County to the pier in San Francisco. A fellow passenger told him the immigration station was off to the right, next to a red-roofed power station. In the background, dark green trees — pines, oaks, cypress and cedar – covered the hills to the water's edge.

Though he looked, he was not sure if the small group of buildings he saw was indeed the former quarantine and detention center from immigrants.

Seeing the island stirred his emotions. More than 60 years before, his mother, alone with four children – the youngest only five-months-old – had come through that center. He had to visit the island himself, maybe experience just a tiny bit of what his mother had gone through.

A few days later, on visiting the island, he learned that the old administration building where the medical examinations were given had burned down in 1940. The immigration station then was moved off the island into the city. Four pairs of pilings, weathered gray on top and green with seaweed at water level, extended at intervals of about 25 yards out into the bay, and were the last remains of what had been the landing deck.

A roughly-hewn granite obelisk, about five foot high, now stood in a flat, grassy area where the old administration building had been. Chinese writing on the stone's one polished surface, paid homage from today's China Town to its earlier generations. A few short steps from the left-over pilings of the former landing dock a replica of the Liberty Bell hung from a frame made of two-by-eight boards over a bronze commemorative plate.

But it was not until he went into the old, three-storied, wooden quarantine building, one of the original buildings which had housed the immigrants that he felt what it may have been like so many decades before when his mother had arrived with her four children. The quarantine building stood on the side of a nearby hill, the yellow paint on its outside had faded long ago. A rusting metal fence topped with barbed wire still girded the building. Each floor had large dormitory rooms, one of the left for women and children, the one on the right for men. The rooms now were bare except for gray, zinc-coated pipes to which bunks, four for each tier, once had been attached, like the bunks in the stinking hold of a troopship.

Even after all the years the building had stood empty, he could smell dust and urine. He wondered how many tens of thousands had sweated and worried in what had to be extreme discomfort as they waited to be cleared for formal entry into the United States. Scratched on the walls – colored a dull blue-green on bottom, a flaked beige white on top – were messages in Chinese and Japanese: some of hope, some of despair. His mother never mentioned how long she and the children had to stay at the quarantine station, but his brother had told him it had been for several days.

He could recall his mother talking about going through the quarantine line. She was awed by the white-skinned doctors and nurses, who seemed so tall, had such big noses, smelled of cheese and spoke a language she didn't understand.

She mentioned being scared. She had overheard the man in front of her talking about people being detained for weeks – some even being sent back to Japan because their papers were not in order. She mentioned worrying; she spoke no English – suppose some questions had been raised about her passport. How was she to respond to those strangers who seemed so impersonal, spoke only among themselves, made her feel as if she and the children were furniture to be examined for any defects before being allowed in?

She had told Jo of being worried. Send her back to Japan? Surely they wouldn't. But she had no way of really being sure. He could picture his mother – struggling with a baby in one arm, the other children clinging to her kimono as she stood in line nervously feeling in her purse to make their passport was still there.

When Jo walked outside of the old immigration building, he immediately sensed the fresh smelling air as he walked back to the former landing-area site. Clear water lapped over clean sand. Two cabin cruisers were anchored only a few dozen yards off shore. A man and a woman were swimming off of one of the cruisers; a man and two young boys were fishing off of the other.

Then he realized how beautiful Angel Island is.

About the Author

Born in Tokyo in Jan. 5,1924, the author arrived in San Francisco on June 21,1924, ten days before the effective date of the Oriental Exclusion Act, and is an *Issei* but of the median age of the *Nisei*. When the *Nisei* were being drafted during WWII, he volunteered when he got out of a "Relocation Center" but was rejected as an "enemy alien." After WWII, as *Nisei* veterans were resettling into civilian life, he volunteered for the U.S. Army because he was going to be drafted.

All this aside, his experiences were common to both generations — grew up on truck garden farms in what is now "Silicon Valley," but was then called the "Prune Capital of the World," lived in a horse stable in Santa Anita and barracks at "Heart Mountain," topped sugar beets, dug ditches, harvested peas in Wyoming, Montana and Washington State, then returned to college, worked on a small town newspaper in Ypsilanti, MI, then was a U.S. soldier in occupied Japan and in Korea during the "Police Action" there.

He then went to graduate school at Columbia University in New York to learn more about Japan, and returned to Tokyo as a newsman to try to be (but did not succeed in being) an "ordinary Japanese." From Tokyo, he went to London with the now-defunct United Press International. In London, most people could not understand why he had an American accent. Even fellow U.S. citizens away from America too long to realize America included peoples from everywhere were confused by his accent.

He transferred from UPI in London to Washington, D.C.; left them to become press secretary for U.S. Senator Hiram Fong from Hawaii, then worked as an information specialist for Occupation Safety and Health Administration (OSHA) until he retired in 1995.

He married a Japanese while in Tokyo where their first son was born; they had a daughter and son born in London. He now has four grandchildren — two who are of Japanese-German descent, two of Japanese-Norwegian descent. After almost two decades as a widower, he met a Shanghai-born, Chinese-American widow, a retiree from the U.S. Agency for International Development.

He now, outside of being pampered and scolded by his wife, raises truck garden crops for food and fun in the garden of neighbors, Dr. Warren and Betty Tsuneishi; enjoys fishing, travels a bit, but basically is just goofing off.

Breinigsville, PA USA
18 March 2011
257951BV00002B/1/P